Oliver is a diverse genre writer. He has written western, crime mystery, thriller, drama and fiction!

When it comes to writing stories, he always focuses on the main key, the plot: and to have a plot you have to have a villain, so he always come up with an antagonist first in every story! To him, villains are the keys to everything in stories and movies 'cause without villains, there's no hero either.

Writing helps him think. He has always loved writing and always will. No matter what genre or story he writes, all his books are based with different types of opinions, deep in thought, which makes them very interesting to read. A lot of the time he adds his own feeling, emotions and opinions into his characters whether it's the villain or the hero.

Oliver Nolan

EX-COP

AUSTIN MACAULEY PUBLISHERS™

LONDON · CAMBRIDGE · NEW YORK · SHARJAH

A CIP catalogue record for this title is available from the British
Library.

ISBN 9781528996372 (Paperback)
ISBN 9781528996389 (ePub e-book)

www.austinmacauley.com

First Published (2020)
Austin Macauley Publishers Ltd
25 Canada Square
Canary Wharf
London
E14 5LQ

In 1989, it was a late afternoon in London and the police department were working flat out to stop any crime that was happening in their city. Barry was on his chair staring at his computer with his arm leaned on his desk. Barry was so quiet and was dead still like a statute; he was having flashbacks on his last crime chase when he met drug dealer Maverick Loki, who he almost caught until Loki managed to escape.

Ever since then, Barry has kept thinking about that day, as he felt so guilty and that he had let his department down. And also let himself down because he thought that he should've caught Loki that day as he is now on the move. Suddenly, Barry jumps out of his skin as his boss, Glen Collins, clicks his fingers in front of Barry's face.

"No time for flashbacks, we have got work to do!" he said. Glen Collins was the Chief Constable of the Metropolitan Police department; he would do anything that he could to make sure that all his colleagues did all that they could to stop any crime from developing in their city.

"What do you think you're doing?" Glen asked as he glared right at Barry's face showing displeasure. He called Barry into his office to have a quiet word with him, so Barry followed Glen into his office and shut the door behind him.

Barry sat with Glen at his desk looking directly face to face at each other.

"Listen, Barry!" Glen said, "I know how desperate you were to catch Loki that time, we all were, but unfortunately we failed. But you can't keep beating yourself up like this Barry, it wasn't your fault that he escaped. The only way we'll do this is if we work together and do it properly. We've got a meeting in a second, now am I going to have to ask another officer to do the talking for you whilst you sit here kicking yourself or are you going to come and do this?" Glen headed to his door to get ready for the meeting and then as he opened the door, he slowly turned his head towards Barry and said to him, "No one can expect to achieve something the first time Barry, that's how we learn to do things properly."

The meeting was about to start and all the fellow officers were sitting down on a banked chair in the briefing room. They were all chatting away to each other without any care whilst they were waiting for Chief G Collins to arrive. As soon as the chief walked in the room, the noise slowly started to reduce but there was still some noisy shuffling going on as the officers were struggling to get comfortable in their seats.

Glen presented himself to the officers standing right in front of the information board with the notes in his hand. "Thank you, OK then listen up!" he shouted, waiting for the room to be silent. As soon as all the officers were quiet, he started to speak and he said to them, "OK! First, I'd like to tell you all how much I appreciate you being here. All the time and effort all of you have put into this community, working flat out day and night to keep our city safe from crime. All the criminals we've captured so far team, take that as a challenge cause mark my words, the biggest is yet to come! I'm going to hand you over to our detective Barry, who's going to tell you all what we're up against."

Barry stood up heading towards the boards carrying photos in his hand. He stuck them onto the board as he started to speak to the officers. "This is our target suspect, Maverick Loki, he's 39 years old and known to be one of the biggest drug smugglers in the country. He was 14 years in prison at the age of 18 for dealing drugs and now since his release he has become a dangerous criminal, leading one of the biggest drug-dealing gangs, smuggling all sorts of illegal substances around the country."

"A warning, ladies and gentlemen, this man is not going to be easy to catch. He is a very dangerous man; you must prepare yourselves at all time, you'll never know what you're up against with him. But when we find him and take him down, we can put an end to these low life drug gangs and tell them once and for all that they are not welcome in our city!"

Barry put another photo up on the board but this time, of a woman who was a relative of Loki, "This is Whitney Naver, she is 36 years old, known to be the current partner to Loki. She lives in Fulham, 23 Viera Road. If we can get enough info from her, then that might help us in catching Loki. Any questions?" He asked the officers and he got one hand up from his mate PC Carl Lawson.

"Didn't she try to call us about a month ago?" he asked, and then Barry admitted that Carl was correct.

"Yes, she did, but when we answered, she hung up the phone. Whether she was deliberately wasting our time to wind-up the police or she was being threatened, they didn't know. But I've got a sneaky suspicion that someone stopped her from calling us, someone who obviously didn't want her to get through to us, and whoever this was I reckon he was the one who put the line down, not her. We are going to pay Ms. Naver a visit tomorrow for a private chat, if we can get some sense into her then maybe she can help us and give us some information that we need. If she helps us, then maybe we can help, and find out what's really going on."

When the meeting was over, all the officers left the room whilst Barry took the photos off of the notice board. Glen Collins went over to Barry and praised him for his work.

"Nice job Barry," he said, giving him a pat on the shoulder. A few hours later when Barry had finished, he drove back to his home in Sidcup. He packed his stuff and got changed then went over to see his delightful friend Michelle, who lived just a few doors down the road from him. Barry knocked on the door and waited. When Michelle answered the door, Barry's heart pounded, he looked at Michelle and gave her a smirk before he said hello.

"Barry! How lovely to see you, so what do I owe the pleasure of your company?" Michelle asked, and Barry just told her that he just came to see her and see if she was ok. Michelle invited Barry into the house and offered him a cup of tea. Barry went into the house and the moment he stepped into the living room, he saw a little baby.

Barry sat on the sofa and watched the kid whilst waiting for Michelle to bring him his tea. Michelle brought Barry his drink and Barry asked her who the baby was. "Who is this little fellow?" Barry asked, and Michelle told Barry that the child was her son, Lucas. Barry asked Michelle where his father was and Michelle told Barry that she was a single mum.

"My ex-boyfriend, Jake Confley, I had been with him for eight months. One night we slept together and a few weeks later I felt sick, very weak and it wasn't long until I found out that I was pregnant. I couldn't wait to tell Jake the news, I thought he'd be delighted, but as soon as I told him he got angry and he left the house. The following day he texted me saying that we were over, he didn't want to be a father, so he dumped me. Now all I'm focused on is this young man."

Barry was sorry to hear about Jake, but was also pleased that Michelle was doing well for herself. He told her that if she ever needed help with anything, he was always there. When Barry finished his tea, he said thank you to his friend Michelle as he headed for the door. Michelle showed Barry out and before he left, he gave Michelle a hug.

On the next day, the police paid a visit to Whitney Naver's house in Fulham. The police were only a few yards away from the house, just entering the road and straightaway they could hear this loud music pumping away. They saw the house with the lights all on and the volume of the music was so loud, it was like maximum volume, high enough to blow the roof off.

Barry was on the scene with his mate PC Carl Lawson and also PC Derek Stan. They knocked on the front door and waited but no one was answering. PC Stan then looked through the living room window and could see two men inside lying on the couches, they looked drunk. There were empty bottles of alcohol inside and lots of cigarettes on the table.

The police then banged on the door with more force to try and get someone to answer. A young woman opened the door and as the police saw her, she looked confused. Her eyes only were half open and every time the police asked her a question, she struggled to answer, mumbling while she answered.

She let the police into the house and Barry straightaway went into the living room to turn the music off.

Barry turned off the music and said, "Right everyone, the party's over!"

But one of the guys wasn't accepting that.

"Who do you think you are distracting our party?" Mike asked Barry in tempered manner, and as soon as he saw the cops entering the room he froze. The whole room exploded, as Mike and his assistant Howe jumped off of the couches and held their knives up against the police. Mike went red in the face and shook like a jelly as he knew that he was about to be taken in. The police got their guns out aiming them straight at the two men warning them that if they didn't drop their weapons the police had the right to shoot, as they were causing threat to the police.

"Don't make it any harder for yourselves guys!" Barry said, but then Mike just struck his knife and attempted to attack PC Carl, but he missed and was arrested. After watching Mike get arrested and seeing two guns pointed at him, Howe knew that now it was life or death. He dropped his knife and gave himself up to the police.

Barry arrested Howe and both the guys were taken in. As they took the guys out of the house, Mike glared nastily at Whitney and gave her a threat.

"You! Don't think you'll get away with this, when he finds out you'll be dead, you hear me dead!"

Barry took Howe's mobile out of his coat pocket and handed him over to PC Derek.

While PC Carl and PC Derek took the two guys into the car to take them to the station, Barry stayed in the house to have a chat with Whitney. Barry thought to himself that he might as well stay and talk to Whitney in the house and save the hassle of waiting for another police car to arrive as they knew it wouldn't be good to take her with the other two men.

Barry told Whitney to have a seat on her couch as he wanted to have a word with her. He fetched her a glass of water to dilute the alcohol down so she would feel better to speak.

"So, you going to tell me what's going on, Whitney?" Barry asked, but Whitney was too scared to say anything. He told her that the more she hides the truth the more this will keep carrying on, but Whitney didn't see anything changing even if she did.

"What's the point? You're not going to do anything; the police say they'll protect us, save us all from crime. Then the first thing you do is come to us asking questions giving us hope that you catch these criminals. But what happens? Nothing. They're still on the loose. So why should I trust you?"

Barry explained to her that she maybe couldn't trust the police but she could trust him.

"Whitney, I understand every word that you've just said there, honestly I do, and I agree with you. It's the police policy, I've argued with my boss about this load of times in his office. They go asking questions to the victims of the crime and then have to write more and more info down, scouting around places to find more clues and scenes of the crime."

"But what for? When it's on camera anyway. And the forensic science team can just get the DNA proof, it's that simple. Once we have proof, we should be out there catching these low life scums, there is no need from all this documentation business. Whenever we do that, we're leaving more criminals loose in the public world for more innocent people to get harmed. But if you tell me what is going on, I promise you whatever it is I can help you, you have my word, trust me."

Then Whitney looked at Barry and asked him why she should trust him, how he was any different to the other police, and Barry then said to her, "I won't tolerate innocent people getting harmed in our community. Whatever it is I will not rest until I have put these low lives where they belong. People like them don't belong here, they should be locked up. But because we're not doing enough about it, more people are getting hurt. I can protect you, but all you got to do is trust me, and tell me the truth."

After hearing the words from Barry, Whitney had a slight feeling that there was something different in him to the other police. Deep down, her thoughts questioned her on whether to trust him or not as she knew this was a risk she was taking. But she knew that if she didn't do something, more and more of the gangsters would keep coming and she wouldn't have any chance in having her life back.

"You do know you're currently under our books as well as your Loki's girlfriend?" Barry said, but then, Whitney just laughed as she said to him,

"Girlfriend! Don't make me laugh, is that what they've be saying to you? I was his girlfriend but only for a short period until I realised what he wanted me for, just to control me and getting me to deal drugs. I told him that I couldn't do it, I told him straightaway that he either stopped the drugs or I'd break up with him.

"But he was never going to stop dealing; he was too addicted to it, the money, the drugs and the hatred. So then I ended it with him, but that hasn't made any difference. Ever since I ended it with him. He gave my address to some of his gang members and now they use my house as their own as a party venue. They bring drinks, and take drugs in my house, it's hell! It happens almost every week and the worst thing is they won't leave until about two o'clock in the morning. They leave my house in an absolute tip, as you just saw, for me to clean up in the morning. Also, there have been days where they have come when I haven't been in so they come the following day and have a go at me for it, thinking that I am deliberately trying to avoid them or trying to call the police"

Barry asked Whitney how long this had been going on and she told him that this had been going on for over six years and Barry was shocked. He questioned himself in his mind how she put up with this for so long, but then knew that it was all in the past and now it was time to end it all. He got his notepad out with his pen and gave Whitney his mobile number and said, "Alright, here's my contact number, if anything else happens you let me know straightaway. I'll make sure these guys never set foot in your house again, you have my word."

Later on, back at the station, the police questioned the two dealers in the room. PC Carl and PC Derek interviewed Howe in room one whilst Barry interviewed Mike on his own in room two. Both of the interviews started but the police were getting nothing from the suspects no matter how much they tried. Barry could tell that he was not going to get anything from Mike so he switched off the recorder and ended the interview. Barry gave Mike the most serious look in the eye and said to him, "Do you know what I see when I look in your eyes? All guiltiness and hatred. I see the truth in you, Mike, you may hide it from the police but you can't hide it from me, I will get it out from you one way or another."

When the interview was finished and Mike was taken back to his cell, Barry had a sneaky peak at Mike's mobile and could see that he had received a missed call and a voice message from a man called Vincent, both sent at 12:08 pm which was exactly the time that the police arrived at Whitney's house. Barry listened to the message which turned out to be a threat.

"Mike, answer the god damn phone! You need to hurry up, the police will be heading your way soon. If you don't hurry up, kill the girl and get out of there now!"

After listening to the message, Barry headed down to the cells and asked the officer to open Mike's door. He told the officer that he was going to have a few minutes alone with him. He took the keys from the officer, and went into Mike's cell. Barry closed the door behind him and spoke to Mike.

"You know, Mike, you've surprised me, because when you showed your anger out trying to attack my colleague today, I thought that I could just see nothing but a careless criminal. But now I'm not sure what to think of you, whether you're just some guy scared and being threatened, or if you're really someone just clever enough to hide his true identity."

"By the way, you missed a call today from a man called Vincent, I'd like to know who he is." Barry sat down on the bed next to Mike and asked him, "Is he the one threatening you, are you scared of him? He left two voice messages and in one of them he was threatening you to kill Whitney, did you know that?"

Barry still didn't manage to get anything out of Mike, he just sat there staring at the floor with his mouth zipped. He wasn't going to get anything out of Mike no matter how hard he tried, so then he got off the bed and took his gun out.

Barry had his back turned against Mike whilst he put his suppresser onto his gun; so that no one would hear his gun go off. He said to Mike, "You have one last chance to tell me who is Vincent."

Mike still didn't say a word, so then Barry turned around aiming his gun straight at Mike. Mike just froze.

"What're you doing?" he said in a panic, and Barry said to him, "If it's cause you're scared of being killed that you're not say anything, well then two can play at that game. You think that they're going to kill you because of who they are. But I'm holding a gun straight at you, deep inside you probably feel that when you've told me they'll finish you off, but if you don't, I'll kill you now on this spot, so you don't really have a choice."

Mike was sure that Barry was bluffing just to get him to talk. He said to Barry, "You won't do it, you're just trying to take me for a fool so I can talk. You're a copper you can't kill!"

Then Barry started losing his temper.

"Is that so?" he said, before he pointed the gun towards the wall and pulled the trigger. He then pointed the gun at Mike's face and started to raise his voice. "Look at the gun, Mike. Look at the gun! Now tell me, what does it really feel like being threatened?"

Mike was absolutely dead scared, his eyes were locked on the gun and his breathing started to pound in terror.

Barry pulled back the firing pin with his thumb setting the gun ready to shoot.

"Now, I'm going to count to three, Mike, and if you haven't started talking this will be the last discussion you've ever had."

As Barry started counting, Mike just lost his patience and couldn't handle it any longer. He shouted to Barry, "Alright, alright, I'll talk. Just please put the gun away."

Barry put down his gun and sat back down on the bed listening to Mike. Mike said to him, "Vincent is not the man that I'd like to get on the wrong side of, he can be a real hard arrogant man, and when he's arrogant he can turn real nasty. But the thing about Vincent is he doesn't realise what he's up against. He's so selfish, and does not think of anything that stands in his way, it's just him. It's like he feels he's a king, when we try telling him he takes it as an offence."

"What do you mean what he's up against?" Barry asked Mike, and Mike explained.

"Vincent used to deal with one of the biggest drug-dealing criminals of all in the UK, Loki. Vince was one of Loki's trade dealers until one day the money just over powered Vincent and he felt that there was no need for him to be working for someone else, he wanted to make his own company, so he betrayed Loki. Vincent lost money once on the trade and ever since he's pointed the finger at Loki, thinking that he robbed him. That's why he keeps sending us threatening messages to kill his ex-girlfriend Whitney."

"But what's you killing Whitney got to do with all this? What's he want you to kill her for?" Barry questioned, and Mike said, "Because it's his ideal plan on getting his own back on Loki. Yes, Loki might not care about the girl but the one thing what Vincent see's is that by killing her anyway, it would punch a hole in Loki's wall, because when the police know about it, the first person that they'll be after is him."

Barry then asked Mike that if Vincent sent him to murder Whitney then why didn't he do it hours before the police arrived on the scene and then Mike admitted to him that he was scared of Loki.

"Did you not get a word that I just said? Vincent I can handle, but Loki, he's a different story mate, he has men everywhere. If he found out that I set him up, god knows what he'd do to me, I wouldn't even like to think."

Barry got up from the bed and looked again on Mike's phone. He searched through his contacts and found Loki's number. When he saw Loki's number on the phone, an idea popped in his mind, he grinned with a smile and then asked Mike, "So if I find Vincent, you recon I'll find Loki?" Mike replied to Barry in a muttering way saying yes, and then Barry just asked Mike if he had any idea where he could find this man Vincent.

Mike told Barry that Vincent ran an old abandoned club in Sutton called the Night Square, he would usually be there every night in the office upstairs. Barry thanked Mike for his help as headed out of the cell and locked the door behind him. On the next day, Barry headed over to the Night Square Club. He went undercover, dressed casually in his black suit and bow tie. He had his grey briefcase with him looking ready for business. He went over to the bar and asked the barman where Vincent was. The barman told Barry that Vince was upstairs in his office so Barry went straight upstairs to find him.

Barry listened carefully through the door and could hear voices inside. In his mind he thought that there must have been about thirteen men in there. Barry needed to think of a way of how to get Vincent without having to get past all his men; he knew that as Vincent was a drug dealer, they were likely to have weapons.

Barry then saw a waitress in front of him cleaning the dirty glasses from the bar downstairs. Barry just lit up with a superb idea; he headed towards the room and waited for the waitress to exit. When the room was empty, Barry got himself an apron and disguised himself as a waitress. He sneaked back downstairs into the bar keeping a close eye out to make sure that no one could see what he was up to. When the coast was clear, he grabbed a champagne bottle out of the freezer and rushed back upstairs. He grabbed the trolley and stuck a load of clean glasses on to it.

Barry opened the champagne bottle and a packet of pills which he had in his pocket. They were rohipnal pills; he dropped one into the bottle and poured the alcohol into the glasses. He put all the glasses onto the table trolley with the champagne bottle and headed to the office. He knocked on the door and walked into the room, pulling the trolley filled with drinks.

He served the gentlemen on the table giving them all a glass of champagne with the bottle. When Barry served all the men on the table, he left the office and took the trolley back to the staff cleaning room. Barry waited outside the door for the room to go silent, it took only three minutes for the men to go unconscious but Barry could hear that Vincent was still awake.

Barry quickly got the hand cuffs out of his case with his gun and hid them in his pocket. He carried the tray in his hand and entered the office listening to Vincent's reaction.

"What the hell have you done to my guys!" Vincent shouted; Barry tried to calm Vincent down as he told him that he doesn't know anything about what happened as he was just serving the drinks. Barry went towards Vincent and when he got close enough, he hit him with his tray. He hit him with full force and hard enough to make him fall off his chair and onto the floor. Fortunately, for Barry, Vincent fell on his front so Barry quickly rushed across to catch him before he tried to get up. As Vincent tried to get up, Barry got his gun and held it at Vincent's head.

"Don't make things any harder!" he said. Barry kept Vincent still and put the handcuffs on.

"Who the hell do you think you are coming here ruining my club!" Vincent shouted, as Barry showed him his ID pass and told him who he was.

"I'm detective Barry Dermative, from the London Police department."

When Barry handcuffed Vincent, he took his phone and got him into the car, Vincent straightaway wondered what he wanted with him.

"You going to arrest me?" Vincent asked. Barry replied to Vincent saying, "That was the plan, why you got any better ideas?"

Vincent just laughed; he said to Barry, "What! better ideas than listening to you, I can think of a few."

Then Barry just shut Vincent up as he gave him the most major answer "Well look who's talking, Vincent you're under arrest for the crime of dealing drugs."

Barry sent a message to Loki from Vincent's phone telling him to meet them at the Shell station at eleven O'clock tomorrow night. Barry showed Vincent the message and he was not amused.

"I see, so this is your idea, is it? Setting me up, he won't answer!" Vincent said, but he was actually proven wrong as it didn't take long for Loki to respond; he sent a message telling them that this better be good.

Vincent started to wonder if Barry knew what he was doing.

"You know this is a booby trap, right? You think you can catch Loki on your own; you're signing your death wish." But nothing was going to stop Barry from catching Loki no matter how many doubts he heard from anyone.

"Do you think I haven't heard that, the same thing over and over again? If you think that, well then some things you've just got to take a risk for, even you should know that. Besides, I won't be on my own." Barry called his colleague PC Carl and told him the news.

"Carl, its Barry, I've arrested Vincent Reed, I'm bringing him in now. Just one thing mate, I'm going to need back up tomorrow evening, including the dogs, we've got a meeting to go to."

Barry took Vincent to the London police station and Vincent was taken to the cells. Carl was still at the police station and Barry told him about what his plan was for tomorrow. Carl told Barry that he would have to mention it to Glen when he gets in tomorrow morning to see if he agrees, but Barry wasn't willing to take the risk as he had certain doubts thinking that if Glen disagreed with his plan then that would mean leaving Loki on the loose.

He said to Carl, "I am not mentioning a word of this to Glen, think about it, if he disagrees to my plan then that means we're leaving one of the most dangerous criminals out in London. That means we're leaving the public in danger and also all these discussions we've been having in the meetings about catching criminals like Loki are a load of rubbish. Tell me something my friend, are we here to do paperwork or are we here to protect the public? I know what I'm here for, what about you? I will catch Loki tomorrow, one way or another, with or without your help."

At 10:30 pm, Carl went over to Barry's house and after a really tough decision to make, he decided to take the risk and help Barry but only because he was his best mate, and Carl had a bit of news for Barry.

"I've managed to call the dog units three of them are willing to help. Also, PC Derek will be with us as well, that's all we have on this."

Barry said thank you to his mate Carl for supporting him, and for being there. But Carl didn't want his appreciation, he warned Barry that he just didn't want to be let down.

"I don't need you to thank me yet, you can thank me when this is done. All I hope is that you're not wasting my time tomorrow, otherwise, I will have wasted these guys' time as well. If it comes to that I don't want to do this but I will report this to Glen."

Barry asked Carl where the dog unit police were and Carl told him that they'll be at the meeting tomorrow at 9 pm in the Dove, including PC Derek.

So, on the following evening after a long day at work, the guys got to the Dove and met up for a discussion. They sat at a table with their drinks and Barry brought a map with him to explain to them how this was going to work. They had exactly 30 minutes to discuss this before they had to go if they were to make this work. Barry opened his book of maps, he looked for the page of London city and explained to the guys what his plan was whilst he pointed to the routes on the pages with his pencil.

"Loki will be expecting to meet Vincent at the Shell in Sutton at Connaught Close, but he won't be expecting our company. Now, this is how it is going to work, Loki will not recognise me as an undercover cop, so I will go in the scene. Carl, you will wait for me outside on Connaught Road, if they make a move for it, you'll know where to follow. PC Derek, you will cover the Westminster Road and dog units, I want you to cover more the south side, near Royston Park, if Loki does attempt to escape from us then that's most likely where he'll be heading."

When the discussion was made and all the officers agreed to the plan, Carl gave them all each a small walkie talkie so that they all could communicate with each other in case there were any problems. It was ten O'clock and the guys drove off to Sutton as quickly as possible, getting to their destinations that they planned. It was 10:45 pm when the guys got to Sutton, Barry texted Loki from Vincent's phone telling him that he was ready and Loki was on his way.

Barry waited for Loki to show up but it wasn't looking like very good news for him as it had reached eleven O'clock and there were no signs of Loki. Carl kept repetitively asking Barry if Loki had shown up but still nothing. It was ten minutes past eleven and Carl was calling it in, he was starting to get annoyed with Barry and told him that he had a lot of explaining to do for wasting police time when they get back in tomorrow.

But suddenly then, Carl saw a BMW car going into the road. He spoke to Barry on the walkie talkie and asked him if this was the suspect coming in now. Barry watched the car approach him and as soon as he saw the man exit the vehicle, he straightaway could tell that it was Loki. Barry contacted his mate Carl and told him that Loki was here. Loki had two other men with him. Barry straightaway got a text from Loki on Vincent's phone, asking him where he was. Barry quickly put his suppressor onto his gun and quickly texted Loki back, as Vincent, telling him that he was on his way.

He got out of the car and headed towards the station. He needed to take down Loki's two assistants if he was to get anything from him. Loki and his gang split up to look for Vincent as they started to wonder if they had been set up. But they had no idea that it was actually Barry who they were looking for.

"Vince, if you think you can play us like this, you'll be making the biggest mistake of your life my friend!" Loki shouted. He told his guys to find Vince and kill him.

The guys split up to find Vincent and Barry now had an advantage, he went after Loki's two assistants, sneaking up as close as he could, and as silently as possible. He followed one of the guys down the alley right behind the Shell store and as there was no CCTV camera around the back so he knew he wouldn't be caught online.

He tapped the guy on the shoulder with his pistol and when the guy turned around Barry just said to him, "Good evening, it's an early night tonight!" Barry knocked the guy out by hitting him hard with his gun. Just a couple of yards ahead Barry saw the other guy heading in his direction. Barry took down Loki's other assistant leaving Loki on his own. It was suddenly all quiet and Loki was really starting to get annoyed.

"You won't get away with this, Vincent. I'll find you, you hear me? And when I do, you'll be sorry!"

But then, Barry approached Loki and told him, "You won't have to worry about that, Vincent is in the cells and you can have your little conversations when you join him!" Barry showed Loki Vincent's phone and proved Loki that it was him that he had been contacting. "Your time is up Loki, there are coppers everywhere surrounding this area. Surrender now and give yourself up." Barry said, but Loki was not going to be that simple.

Loki laughed and said, "You misunderstand me, my friend. The thing you've got to understand about me is I take orders from no one!"

Loki fired his gun at Barry and Barry quickly ran into cover. He held Barry back until he got back into the BMW and drove off. Loki got out of the area and was on the run. Barry quickly contacted Carl to follow Loki and he went straight back into his vehicle.

When Carl got the call, he quickly put his blue flash lights on and turned on the siren. He could see the blue BMW straight ahead of him as it left the road, so Carl stepped on it to catch up with the vehicle and the chase began. Carl then contacted the others on the radio and told them that Loki was on the move, he chased Loki down Connaught Road towards Surrey Grove and straight ahead of him he could see another police car. Loki then just turned his wheel sharp and went down Royston Avenue. However hard it got, he was not giving himself up. But then, half way down the road, Loki could see more blue flashing lights on the road ahead, he knew that he was surrounded. Loki started to panic; he parked his car quickly and ran to Royston Park.

As the police pulled out, they could see Loki running to Royston Park. But it was so late at night and in the park, it was pitch black, there were only a few street lights on at the park including the lights at the nursery. The police dog units got out of their vehicles quickly and released their hounds from the cages, putting them on the leads and getting them to sniff out Loki.

Two dogs were on the scene sniffing out Loki's trail. PC Carl guarded the gate to the park on Royston Avenue to keep an eye in case he tried to come back to the vehicle. Ten minutes later Barry and Derek arrived on the scene. Barry asked Carl where Loki was and Carl said to him, "Loki has run into the park, the dogs are keeping track of him, they'll have him in a bit."

Just then, PC Carl got a response from the dog handlers.

"We've found the suspect, he's in the forest on the run." Barry ran into the forest as fast as he could, he searched in the forest but couldn't find Loki anywhere. He knew he had to be somewhere but as they couldn't find him, Barry had the slight feeling that Loki was hiding. He tried to see if he could get a response from Loki as he started to speak to him loud and clear through the forest.

"Show yourself, Loki, you've got nowhere to run!"

Loki heard Barry and straightaway from the volume of his tone, he could tell that he was close nearby. Loki looked behind the tree and could see Barry approaching. Barry headed towards the tree getting closer and closer, holding his gun in his hand. "You know you're not making it any easier for yourself, Loki. I've dealt with criminals like you before, you think that by waiting around hiding you're wasting police time and the police will just leave so you can escape. But you're wrong, it's your own time you're wasting cause no matter how long it takes we'll find you, and you'll be inside"

Loki – "Oh! Hard words coming from a man who, if I remember rightly, failed to catch me the last time we met."

Barry – "How dare you, you were lucky last time. I was an inch away from catching you until you got over that fence. But that was one mistake which I can guarantee will not happen again!"

Barry – "Come on, Loki, time to step up mate, be a man. All those innocent people you have killed, the lives you have ruined. The least you can do is show a bit of remorse."

Loki – "Oh, and like you haven't, you know what's funny, detective? We're the same, you and I, we're both criminals."

Barry – "What're you talking about? I am not a criminal, I'm nothing like you!"

Loki – "Really! Are you sure about that? You're after me because I'm a killer right. But the truth is detective you kill as well, you kill people that cause danger to the public, so tell me detective what makes you any different?"

Loki – "Do you want me to tell you detective? The only reason people don't see you as a criminal like me is because you're working for the law. Just because the police are by the laws side the public see you as a hero. If you weren't, they'd all want you locked up like the rest of us. But do you know what the best thing is? You spend all your time going out catching criminals and don't realise that you're actually getting mugged. The real criminal around here detective, it's not you, not me, it's the law. They're robbing us all, giving us excuses for improving our country when they're just lies to improve their payslips. Charging us all tax fines, mortgage fines, bills and every year they increase the payment until people are begging on their knees. They don't care about us detective; everything they say is a lie. I say we don't let them get away with this, using us as slaves for the country. Mark my words detective, you earn nothing when helping the law, but you earn a fortune when going against it, the least you could earn is £20,000 for doing drugs, I bet you don't earn half that do you? If they rob us then we rob them, money controls everything, even when it comes to life and death, even you know that."

Barry – "No, people see me as a hero because I don't stop until I know that the public is safe from animals like you!"

Loki laughed behind the tree and then just replied to Barry saying, "Is that so, well then let's find out shall we?" He came out from behind the tree and stood in front of Barry. Barry had his gun pointed straight at Loki, and Loki tried to prove to Barry that he was a criminal. He persuaded Barry to shoot him as he could tell how much Barry hated him.

"Come on then, what're you waiting for? Finish me! End it all for those who have suffered under my hands. You know you're itching to pull that trigger, and see what a hero you will really become."

Barry's eyes closed showing no fear. He pulled the pin on the gun and glared at Loki whilst he held it. Barry could feel the tension, he felt almost so desperate to do it as his finger slowly started to pull the trigger. As the finger got closer to closing in on the trigger, it was only a few seconds until Loki was going to die. Until then, Barry got stopped, he could feel his soul speaking, and inside his mind, he heard his own voice saying, "Don't do it, you're better than that!"

Barry put down his gun and said to Loki, "No, I'm not like you! I'm taking you in, Loki." Barry arrested Loki and took him to his car. He contacted his colleagues and told them that Loki was captured. They took him to the police station and kept him in the cells until they were ready to question him. Barry had a small bag of cocaine which he found in Loki's coat pocket when he arrested him. He put the bag into the evidence room before he left the station and went home.

When Barry got home, he straightaway could see all the letters that he had received from the post. He opened the envelopes and could see that they were more increased bills for him to pay. The electric, water, the gas and also the mortgage. Barry put the letters on the small desk in his living room and got himself a drink of whiskey as he was a bit of an alcoholic; he always had a drink of whiskey whenever he got stressed about something. Barry took a swig of his drink and looked at his bills on the table, straightaway he could hear Loki in his mind repeating to him, "The law is robbing us, Barry, sending us bills, increasing them each year until we end up begging on our knees, they're nothing but crooks!"

After he had finished reading the letters, Barry headed off to bed. He struggled to walk properly as he had got himself wasted. He was very dizzy in the head and struggled to walk properly; he headed upstairs but took a long while to get there. At 8:30 am, the alarm raised and Barry woke up with a banging headache.

He held his hands on his head whilst saying to himself, "I shouldn't have drunk all that yesterday!" He got himself dressed and ready for work, wearing his white shirt and grey suit. He went into the living room to put his tie on whilst he looked at himself in the mirror. When Barry turned around, he saw the envelopes that he put on the desk yesterday and could hear Loki again in his mind, "The law is robbing us Barry, they're nothing but crooks!"

When Barry got himself to work, as he entered the building heading to his desk, he heard his name being called by Glen.

"Barry! Barry! Detective, in my office, now!" Barry followed Glen to his office and shut the door behind him, Barry could tell by the tone of Glen's voice and by the look on his face that he was in trouble.

Glen – "You had to do it again didn't you; you had to disobey me. I thought I mentioned this clearly to all of the team, that we were to take no further actions on Loki until the documents were completed and more evidence were shown. Now I've asked PC Branden who covers my place at night when I'm not here, and he has told me that he didn't know anything about this. So please can you explain what Loki is doing in our cells?"

Barry – "Oh God, listen to yourself, Glen! One day you say you'll do anything to keep crime off the streets, but then in a few days you'll change, having a go at us for catching them all because we haven't done this sodding paperwork. What are we news reporters now, are we? The paper is more important than the people, is it?"

Glen – "I don't have to listen to this, you're on a caution. If you disobey me one more time, detective, then I will have no choice but to give you suspension. Do I make myself clear?"

"Yes, sir," Barry said. He headed towards the door and then stopped. He turned his head and looked at Glen again.

"Is there something you want to say, detective?" Glen asked.

"Oh, it's nothing important, it's just funny the number of people I've spoken to that have doubted the police, I could never understand why, but I managed to give them hope, confidence and every time I did what needed to be done. Now I finally see the truth, you think we're friends to the public? Why should the public respect us if we're not going to do what needs to be done? We're just as bad as the people we're after!" Barry said.

After a long stressful day at work, Barry went home and as he wasn't in the mood for any visitors, he straightaway locked the door behind him. He closed the curtains on all the windows and then went into the cupboard to get a new bottle of alcohol. He sat on his couch in the living room and then just looked at his bills. He sat there staring at his tele listening to his mind. His mind was playing deep down on him as the same voices of negative reactions just kept repeating in his mind, this time not just Loki, but from Glen as well. It just went on and on in Barry's mind and the drink wasn't doing anything, it was only a certain amount of time until Barry's mind just shut off.

It was like Barry had almost been hypnotised and at that moment, something had changed. Barry had woken up into a different man. It was like a grenade had struck in his mind, Barry went Rogue. He put his drink on the floor and straightaway went into the kitchen. He got a small sealable bag out; he got out his flour and then put a hand full into the bag ready for tomorrow as he had a plan to help Loki escape. He rapped the bag up carefully so that the flour wouldn't fall out and he put it in his case with his gun and his hand cuffs ready for work in the morning.

In the morning, Barry got himself ready with his case and went off to work. He got to the London Police Department and straightaway he got on with business. He headed down to the cells and opened the shutter on Loki's door, he spoke to Loki as quietly as possible as he was trying to make a deal with him without anyone hearing.

Barry – "Loki!"

Loki – "Oh. Well if isn't the great detective himself. Come to give me more stick have you? Well, go ahead, I can take it!"

Barry – "I haven't come to abuse you. I've come to talk. Were you actually serious when you said you get £20,000 or more for drugs?"

Loki – "Why would you want to know? All you want is me to suffer, locked up in a cell. And guess what, detective, your wish is coming true!"

Barry – "Maybe I might have had second thoughts!"

Barry – "I have a plan to set you free!"

Loki just laughed; he found it hilarious when Barry said that he could set him free. Loki just wet himself laughing as he found it the most ridiculous joke he ever heard from Barry.

Loki – "You can't be serious; you've been chasing me down for days wanting to catch me. Now suddenly when you catch me you want to set me free. Are you sure you are a copper detective?"

Barry – "Look I haven't got time to stand here and listen to you, I'm here to offer you a deal. You get about £20,000 or over for drugs, don't you? I can get you out of here now, but if I do, I want at least half of the pay. Your choice Loki, stay in here and rot or pay me and be free!"

Loki – "Alright, detective, you win, get me out of here, and then we'll discuss business."

So then, Barry told Loki that he wouldn't be long as he closed the shutter on the door and went undercover. He straightaway headed to the evidence room and looked for the small bag of cocaine that he took from Loki. Barry kept an eye out in case anyone else came into the room, and as soon as he found the bag of coke, he swapped it for his small bag of flour. Barry put the bag of cocaine in his coat pocket and headed up to Glen's office. He knocked on Glen's door and apologised for his behaviour.

Barry – "Sir, I have an apology to make for my behaviour yesterday. I should not have spoken to you in that manner, I am sorry."

Glen – "It's alright, detective, just forget about it now, it's in the past; we all have a bad spell at some point. You've come here and apologised, that's good enough for me!"

Later on, Barry was about to be interviewing Loki with PC Carl. He got the keys to the cells and opened Loki's cell. He put the hand cuffs on Loki and said to him, "Right, here's what's going to happen; I will be interviewing you shortly and when I ask you about that bag of coke you are going tell me that it's flour. We have only one shot at this, whatever other crap you want to come out with I don't care but you must admit to me in the room that it is flour. Don't screw this up; PC Carl will be watching me with Chief Glen so whatever you say they will hear."

Barry took Loki to interview room two and with Glen and Carl watching from the other room, the interview begun. Barry had to ask about ten questions to Loki and from nearly all of them, Loki didn't give any comments. Until on the last question, Barry asked him about the bag of cocaine, so then Loki just turned his head and looked at Chief Glen. He stared at Glen and gave him an evil smirk, as deep in his mind Loki was finding this absolutely wonderful, watching a copper about to betray his own kind. He looked at Barry and told him that it was just plain flour in the bag.

When Loki said that it was plain flour in the bag, Carl started getting concerns. He asked his boss Glen what they were supposed to do with Loki now as he had the slightest feeling that he was up to something.

PC Carl – "There's something he's not telling us, I'm sure of it. Why would he just be hanging around with other dealers carrying a bag of ordinary flour? It doesn't make sense."

Chief Glen – "I know it doesn't, I agree with you that there's something he's not telling us, or something he's planning.

But without evidence, we can't risk taking further action. We have no choice; we have to let him go."

Glen told Barry to finish the interview and straightaway Loki was let out. Barry walked Loki outside the front and when no one was watching he quickly dragged Loki to the side of the building and pinned him to the wall.

Barry – "Right, a deal's a deal, I've got you out. Now, where's my money?"

Loki – "You really think this is the right time to be doing this, detective? Right outside your police station? You could be getting us both in trouble."

Barry – "This may be the only time I get anything from you."

Loki – "Oh! I see, you don't trust me because I'm a criminal. You think everything that I say will be a lie and that I will just run off."

Loki – "Meet me tonight at the Cargo club, 10:30 pm and we'll discuss business."

Barry – "Yeah! And what makes you think I'd do that? How can I trust you? How do I know this won't be you trying to set me up?"

Loki – "Like you said, a deal's a deal, You offered me freedom and you did it, now it's only right for me to return the favour. You meet me at the Cargo club and we'll talk business."

Barry let Loki go and went back into the station. Later on in the evening, Barry got Loki's bag of cocaine out of his coat pocket and made himself a cigarette. Barry took his first puff and straightaway he could feel the burn from the powder going through his nose. His face started going red, it was like his face was on fire. At 9:45 pm, Barry left his house and headed to the Cargo night club. He had his case with his notepad, pen and torch inside, but he left his gun behind with his badge. He got to the nightclub at 10:25 pm and straightaway could see Loki standing outside the building with two men beside him. He went to Loki and Loki introduced him to his troops Luis and Duran.

Loki – "Ah, here he is just the man I was mentioning to you guys, Barry Dermative. Barry, may I introduce you to my colleagues Luis and Duran. Boys, this is the detective who helped me escape."

Barry – "Enough with chit-chatting, Loki. I just came here to collect my money and leave. When I'm gone you can do as much talking as you like."

Loki – "Oh yeah, I forgot you were a very impatient man, detective. The thing is, detective, I never really said that I'd pay you for my release; I said I'd discuss business. However, I suppose a reward is deserved."

Loki gave Barry £500 in cash for his release, and then he gave Barry two bags full of Rock. He told Barry that the bags needed to be delivered to Larson who was one of Loki's closest companions. Loki told Barry that Larson was not a man who would tolerate nonsense; if Barry could sell the drugs to Larson then he'd be in the club and be earning a fortune.

Loki – "I promised Larson that I'd have it delivered to him by midnight; I'm counting on you Barry to do the job for me. When you've done that Barry, you can forget taxes, forget your fees. You'll be a changed man; you'll feel like a king!"

Barry asked Loki where he was supposed to find Larson and Loki told him it was in the Waitrose car park in Harrow Weald. So then Barry made his way to the to the supermarket in Harrow Wealth and when he got there, he could straightaway see that everywhere was empty, the only thing he could see was a group of men with a white van, but he had been spotted as well.

Barry drove as close to the van as he could, thinking of the easiest solution. As Barry pulled the brakes, straightaway he heard the gun pins clicking one by one. As he looked out the window, he could see five men with their guns pointed straight at him. The guys were Larson's men, and they straightaway could tell who Barry was. Barry quickly grabbed the bag, got out of the car and walked towards the gang.

Larson – "Well, look who we have here, boys? If it isn't the great detective himself. You've got some front coming here on your own! Kill him!"

Barry – "Wait, don't shoot! I'm unarmed, I come alone. I've got a delivery to hand over by the order of Loki."

Larson and his gang just laughed, as they knew that Barry and Loki were bad nemesis, and straightaway after hearing that from Barry they were sure that they were being tricked.

Larson – "You! with Loki? Do me a favour, he hates your guts, I'm sure you properly hate his as well. Nice try, Barry. This is another one of your tricks, there's probably cops on their way now, but bad luck detective because they won't catch us, all they'll see is a dead copper lying here on the streets!"

As the guns clicked pointing at Barry, Larson asked him if he had any last words to say. But then Barry just threw the bag of drugs in front of Larson and told him to look inside. Larson opened the bag and could see that Barry was telling the truth as there was 6 big bags of Rock inside, which he was owed from Loki.

Larson – "You're deadly serious?"

Barry – "I never lie."

Larson – "Is that so, well let's find out now, shall we? In this small bag in my hand is £50,000 in cash. Now, I am willing to pay now for the drugs, but first, you must prove to me that this is not set up and that you are one of us?"

Larson gave the bag of money to his colleague and asked Barry to come over as he grabbed one of the bags of rock and cut it open with his knife. He then gave Barry a rollup. Barry went over to Larson and looked into the bag of rock; he took the rollup from Larson and went straight into action. He held the rollup into the bag quickly without any hesitations and breathed in the drug. Barry could feel the drug going through him; it was so strong, burning his nostrils but he wasn't going to let that affect him.

He gave the rollup back to Larson and just acted normal, although the drug was still harming him, he just acted as a hard man waiting for Larson to give him his money. Larson just said to Barry, "Well, I guess that explains the answer!"

He got the money from his colleague and gave it to Barry, as he shook his hand and said to him, "Welcome to the club, Barry, ex-cop!" Barry took the money and headed straight back home. As the days went by Barry got more and more into the drugs. He became a totally different man.

The money he was earning had brainwashed him and the drugs he took were just filling him with joy and confidence. Barry carried on doing his work at the London Police department through the days before doing his business with Loki at nights so that nothing suspicious would be noticed by the police. But when Barry had boxes given to him by Loki for him to sell, Barry started getting concerns as he didn't really like the idea in having drugs inside his house, he straightaway opened one of the boxes in his house and saw four bags of cocaine inside. Barry hid the box in the loft so that it wouldn't be found, however, he took one of the cocaine bags out and started to smoke a joint each day. But it was only 2 weeks until Barry's addiction to cocaine got really bad, as he now smoked 6 joints every day a week. Barry's addiction to drugs just got out of control that he got so ill from it, he had to call in sick from work at the police department for a week. The same excuse came on the following week and this started to concern Chief Glen and he wondered why Barry would just suddenly call in sick for two weeks.

Also, what made it even more curious for Chief Glen was that on both the times Barry called in sick he didn't give the same reason for being ill. Glen expected Barry to come in on the following Monday, he kept his eyes at the door to see if Barry came in but there were still no signs of him. When the clock reached 11 am and Barry was an hour late for work, Glen could tell that this was going to be another day of him not showing up. He got on the telephone in his office and started calling Barry constantly to try and get through to him, but no matter how much he tried, he got no answer.

Glen really started losing his patience with Barry and started to think that Barry had just been calling in sick as an excuse. He asked PC Carl to go and pay a visit to Barry's house after work and see what he was really playing at. So when he finished work at 8 pm, he got changed and locked his uniform inside. Carl headed for his car in the staff car park and drove off to Barry's house. When Carl got to Barry's house, he could see that all the curtains had been drawn on the windows, he wondered if that meant that Barry was asleep, but he highly doubted it.

Carl knocked on the door but got no answer, so then Carl opened Barry's post and looked through as he tried to call for Barry's attention. But then, the first time Carl opened the post, he witnessed something; through the post he could smell drugs inside the house. Carl called PC Brandon by his mobile and asked for dog units, as the house just stunk of drugs.

Carl – "Hello, Branden, its Carl!"

PC Branden – "Hi Carl, what can we do for you?"

Carl – "I'm at Barry's house, I got asked by Glen to pay him a visit. He doesn't seem to be in at the moment. But there's something strange, all the curtains are drawn and when I looked through his post the house stank of drugs!"

PC Branden – "What type of drugs?"

Carl – "I don't know! cocaine, rock, and cannabis. Something like that? I know there's something in there causing that smell. That's why I was wonder if I could get the dog units to investigate."

PC Branden – "Right, OK, I'll send them over now."

After a 30 minutes wait, the assists arrived. As it was a drug crime suspicion, PC Brandon had to send one dog unit car and one truck of special force police. With Barry still nowhere on site, Carl gets on with the job and searches the property. The police get the dogs out of the vehicle and they knock on the door for the final time to see if Barry answers. With still no answer at the door, they finally realised that they were going to have to use the battering ram.

The police battered Barry's door down and forced their way into the property. The Special Forces searched the whole house holding their machine guns high, they guarded every room of the property whilst the dogs went into business sniffing out for drugs.

Kody, the German Shepherd police dog, was let off the leash and straightaway started sniffing his way inside the house, and it wasn't long until he found a trace. He would sit down facing the location where he found the smell so that the officers would then investigate to find the drugs. Kody found the bag of cocaine that Barry left in the living room drawer as he had been smoking it, and he also sat below the loft staring at the entrance which told the police that there was something aboard.

Carl opened the loft and turned on the light; he straightaway saw a white box in front of him and opened it. On that moment Carl couldn't believe his eyes as he could see 5 more wrapped bags of cocaine and in that moment Carl started to get frustrated.

Carl – "No! No! No! this can't be happening, not Barry!"

Carl calmed his reactions down and asked the officers to search the rest of the house whilst he searches the rest of the loft. But the dog units told Carl that Kody had already searched everywhere in the house apart from the loft and that was all he found. So then Carl searched everywhere in the loft to see if there were any signs of other drugs but there was nothing so the police took the box of the cocaine bags and the bag that was loose. But, just moments later, Barry appeared at his house and he saw the police vehicles outside. Barry had a nervous feeling and wondered what the hell was going on when he saw special force police vehicle at his drive. He went to his house and as he headed for the door, he straightaway noticed that the door had been battered down.

As Barry entered the house, the special force straightaway shouted at him telling him to get down on the ground. They forced Barry to go down on his knees and told him not to move; Carl told the police to leave it to him. So then the Special Forces went outside and left Barry to Carl. Carl started talking to Barry wondering why he would do something so unforgiving.

He told Barry to stand up and talk to him face to face, so then Barry stood right in front of Carl with his head down.

"Look at me, Barry, look at me!" Carl shouted, Barry looked at Carl and they both started to argue.

"Why Barry? What did I ever do to you that would make you think of doing this?" Carl asked Barry.

Barry just replied saying, "You haven't done anything!" But Carl was starting to blame himself for Barry's crime as he felt that there must have been something that he had done to upset him for him to want to go and do this. "Really, you sure about that? Cause from where I'm standing, this doesn't look like that to me. So if it's not me Barry then please do tell what it is!"

Suddenly then, Kody walked towards Barry, he smelt drugs in his coat pocket. Carl saw Kody smelling Barry's pocket and as soon as Kody sat down staring at the jacket Carl could tell that there was something in Barry's pocket. Carl searched

Barry and found a small bag of coke in his pocket and Carl noticed something fishy about the bag. After Carl body searched Barry, he arrested him and put on the handcuffs. He said to Barry that he was under arrest for the suspicion of criminal drug-dealing. The police took Barry to the station and locked him in a cell for the night. Barry now was treated as a prisoner by his own police department. To them he was not a colleague anymore, he was now a criminal.

When Glen found out on the next morning, he was absolutely in shock. He couldn't believe it as he had been betrayed by one of his most loyal and trusted colleagues. PC Carl went into Glen's office and showed him bags of cocaine that Barry had wrapped-up in the box. He also showed Chief Glen the small bag of cocaine that Kody found in Barry's pocket and told Glen what he thought had really happened.

PC Carl – "Sir, this was found in Barry's jacket pocket, I think he's deliberately helped Loki escape. Loki is one of the biggest drug dealers in the UK, why would he just carry a small bag of flour? It doesn't make sense. I think Barry took the real evidence and swapped it for that fake bag of flour, because he knew that without proof we wouldn't take any further charges and Loki would be free."

Chief Glen – "But why would he want to help a criminal like Loki get loose? He always kept saying to me how much he wanted to take him down, now suddenly when he is caught, Barry helps him escape. I'm going to get answers from him!"

Glen went to see Barry down in the cells, he asked the officer to unlock the cell as Glen wanted to go inside. So then the officer opened the door to Barry's cell and Glen went inside to talk to Barry.

"I must say, it gives me great sorrow and anger to think that a former colleague of mine would suddenly turn his back on the community and give his career up for drugs!" Glen shouted.

"Is this cause you can't have it your way, is that it, Barry? Because you have to do so much paperwork and you can't catch criminals the way you want? Is this your idea of getting your own way back on me?" Glen asked in a tempered manner, and then he got a response from Barry.

"Do you ever question yourself, Glen, what the public actually think of the police? One mistake from us and the words spread. They don't see us as their heroes; they just see us as the criminals working for the government, like us against them."

"That's rubbish, you're talking absolute nonsense. Where have you been hearing all this? Is this what Loki has been saying to you? Is that why you helped him escape? You took Loki's drugs from the evidence room and swapped them for a bag of flour because you knew that by taking away the proof that we had we would have to set him free" Glen said. He looked at Barry in the eye and said to him, "I don't know what discussion you had with Loki, but whatever it was I hope you realise what you have done."

Barry – "Oh, and what's that, Glen, hey? Smuggling drugs or releasing Loki? Because if I remember rightly, Loki wouldn't even have been here if it weren't for me. I don't know what you're complaining at cause you didn't even want him in; you had a right go at me for bringing him in, so you should be pleased that I've set him free. You know it's funny, 4 months it took you to catch me out, but only because you knew me as a former colleague. If you didn't know me this would've taken ages. You never would've caught Loki without me, you know it yourself. You want him? Go and get him. He's all yours now. But you know what's really going to happen you're not going to get him, he'll be out for years smuggling drugs doing his usual, while you're sat at your desk in the station searching for proof and doing more and more papers."

Glen had enough of listening to Barry; he asked the officer to open the door and let him out of the cell. As Glen headed for the door, he looked at Barry and gave him his last word, "You had everything you could ever wish for

Barry, a career, friends, more than you could ever wish for. Now you've lost it all, whatever Loki's said to you was a lie, he's brainwashed you, and now he's made you lose everything. Don't you see, Barry? He's set you up and put you right on his spot, getting you locked up whilst he's out loose."

Glen left Barry and straightaway headed back to his office. He filled in the forms and contacted the Old Bailey court. Barry would have to stay in the cells until the court were able to set him a date for his court case. After a day or two, Glen received a message from the court telling him that they had set a date for Barry's case on April 22nd 1989 which was a month away, so that meant Barry had to stay in the cells for another 4 weeks before going to court. After a month's wait, the day had finally come and Barry was escorted from the police station to the Old Bailey. It was 9:30 am and the case was to start at 10 am. So, with only 30 minutes left, Barry waited in a small room until he was to be taken up. But then, someone came in and introduced herself to Barry.

"Hello, Barry Dermative, I'm Reni Bellisa, your lawyer for today's court. If there's anything you have to say, anything they say that is not true you have the right to speak. I'll be here to defend your case."

Barry told Reni that he had nothing to say, so then Reni left Barry and headed to the court room. Twenty minutes later Barry was shown to the court room by the ushers and taken to the stand. He took his place on the witness stand, waiting for the judge and jury to arrive; he could see all his police colleagues and his friend Michelle in the audience. Chief Glen was waiting on the dock as he was going to be answering questions on Barry. The judge and jury arrived on the scene and the case was about to begin. Barry looked at the judge as he watched him take his place, wearing his big red robe and his long-pointed judge wig.

James Baldwin was the judge who was taking Barry's case today; he put his glasses on and looked at the forms that he received from the police.

"So, Barry Dermative, an undercover police officer, you're in court today for the conviction of smuggling drugs," said Judge Baldwin. The judge handed the speech over to Luke Johnson, the prosecutor and he started asking questions to Barry about what he had done.

Luke Johnson – "Thank you, your honour! Now, Barry Michael Dermative, 39 years old, a former police detective, member of the London Police Department. Sounds like a great career you had here, Barry. What made it go so wrong?"

Barry – "No comment!"

Luke Johnson – "By the look of these statements you never got on very well with your boss. You always had a disagreement with Chief Glen is that right?"

Barry – "Well yes, me and Glen did have our moments occasionally, but who doesn't? Everyone has a disagreement."

Luke Johnson – "But did that suddenly struck you; not having it your way so you decided to betray the police force and commit crime? Something must have really hit you hard to want to do this Barry, you tricked your own colleagues to help a criminal escape didn't you?"

When the prosecutor kept going on at Barry, tempers started to rise and all the fingers were getting pointed at him. But then, Barry's defendant Reni, stepped in asking questions to Glen and Carl who were confronting him.

Reni – "So, Glen Joshua Collins, 56 years old, head of the London Police Department, also known as the metropolitan police, the main police force in London. You say you would do anything to keep the public safe from crime, but I have a solution. If you want to keep the public safe from crime, surely you should be out there catching them as you say. Isn't that your job, Mr Collins?"

Glen – "Well, we do everything that we can. We have the hardest working police force in the UK, we work flat out day and night to protect the public from criminals."

Reni –"Now you see, that's where you're giving me doubts! You keep saying you'd do anything to keep the public safe from crime, but the truth is Glen, the paperwork is more important to you isn't it? You had a go at Barry here for bringing a criminal into the station without your permission; you took him into your office and gave him a caution. So can you explain that to me? Because by the sounds of things to me, the only person who really wanted to keep the public safe from crime was Barry?"

Glen – "That is! That is unfair; I have done all that I can to keep our capital safe from crime. Do you known how much courage and progress it took for me to get to this stage as a head of the London Police? I cannot help the way the rules are made for the police force, but when they're there then we must obey by them. Barry was one of my most trusted companions; he was the best man for catching criminals. Every time I sent him out, he was like a dog fetching a bone. But Barry never would obey by the rules, and we used to always argue about it. He would refuse to do the papers if anything came up. The one thing that Barry doesn't realise is, he wouldn't still have had this job if it weren't for me, I kept him in the police force just because how brilliant he was at the job. How he was so determined, fearless, and would just catch any criminal down."

When Judge Baldwin had heard enough from the courtroom, it was time to make a decision on whether to sentence Barry or not. The judge asked the twelve people in the jury and every one of them found Barry guilty, so then the hammer went down and Barry was sentenced to seventeen years in prison for smuggling drugs.

After hitting the hammer, the judge looked at Barry and said to him, "So, Barry, you've lost your job, your friends, your home, your career! Seventeen years is a long time, maybe it'll give you the chance to think about what you have done!"

The trial ended and Barry was taken to the HMP Pentonville and with no help on the line for his drug addiction, Barry was going to have to put up with it throughout his stay.

After spending 17 long horrible years in prison, Barry's freedom had finally come. As he got taken from the cell, the guards gave Barry his clothes and led him to a room where he was able to get changed. Barry got changed in the room and handed back the prison shirt before he exited the building.

As Barry got out of the building, he could see his friend Michelle waiting for him outside in the carpark. She was going to give Barry a lift back to Sidcup. Barry entered the vehicle and Michelle asked Barry how he felt after finally coming out of jail.

"How do you feel? You must feel pleased that you're finally out of that horrible place?" But after seventeen years behind bars, everything had just flushed away from Barry.

From all that time in prison, his drug addiction managed to drain away, but so did his faith. Barry didn't feel anything, except total shame. He felt that he had flushed away his lifestyle on the day he committed crime as he answered Michelle saying, "It makes no difference if I'm in or out of prison. This doesn't change anything to what I have done. I've ruined my entire life!"

Michelle took Barry to her house and invited him in for a drink, as she felt that he needed some company. Michelle was a really close friend to Barry; she was the only person who went to visit Barry in prison when she could because she had known Barry for so long and deep down she knew that he was a good man.

Michelle gave Barry a cup of tea and tried to talk sense into him telling him not to feel as if his life was over. Barry thanked Michelle for the tea and apologised to her for raising his voice at her in the car on the way as he felt rude to do so.

Michelle – "You shouldn't be so hard on yourself like this, thinking your life is over, because it isn't. Yeah you made one big mistake, but everyone makes them. You took seventeen years' punishment for that. Now you can move on, start fresh, have a new beginning!"

Barry – "If only it were that simple though, Michelle. I was a detective once; I loved every moment of that job, chasing criminals, being a hero. But now it's all gone, because of my one foolish mistake, and there's no turning back. Now I'm stuck for the rest of my stupid life holding records in my hands!"

Michelle – "If your job really meant that much to you then why did you do it, why did you take drugs?"

Barry – "I don't know, I guess because of greed and I suppose part of it was to get my own back on Glen at the time. When I caught Loki, the things he said to me just went into my head; it was like I believed him. I was struggling to pay bills, mortgages and rent. Although I loved the job, I wasn't earning enough, I needed more money, and it just all got together in my head. Glen, Loki, the bills. It was too much pressure on my mind, and then I just thought if I tried once on the drugs, just once to get my own back on Glen, to earn the cash that I needed, then maybe I'd get away with it. But anyway, I'm sure you didn't bring me here to talk about my story. What do you need me for?"

Michelle told Barry that she just came to see if he was OK after his long time in prison, but Barry could tell by the tone of her voice that was not true and that there was something she wasn't telling him.

"Oh come on, Michelle, I can tell by the look on your face that's not true. Something's bothering you, isn't it? And you need my help, don't you?" Barry said.

Michelle could tell that Barry wasn't silly, and she straightaway confessed what it was she needed his help with. She told him that she was worried about her boy Lucas.

Lucas was now a grown adult but was still living with his mum, and no matter how old he got, she could never stop worrying about him as he was the only child she had. She had the feeling that Lucas was in trouble, in some sort of situation as whenever he went out after school, he would always end up coming back home harmed.

Michelle – "Everyday he goes out after school and I never know when he's coming back. It seems to get later and later. He refuses to answer his phone and whenever he does eventually come back home, he's always in a terrible state. He comes back either bruised, black eyed, scared. He even once came back with a bad cut on his arm. Whenever I ask him what's going on, he won't say anything to me and he just goes straight to his room. It's like he's too scared to say anything. I'm just so scared that one day something really bad will happen to him, and I'll get a call from the hospital watching him end up in a coma or dead."

Barry – "Have you tried calling the police?"

Michelle – "I can't call the police, what good will that do? If this is some sort of gang he's got himself into, then if I call the police, it will just make things worse for him and for me. The first thing the police will do is come here and ask me questions, when I have no idea on what's going on. Also, if I did that and he is involved, then I would lose him. Please Barry, you're really the only person I know that can help, find him for me. Whatever situation he's in, get him out and bring him home safety?"

Barry – "Don't worry, Michelle. I'll find him, you've been there for me throughout the years whenever I was in trouble. If it weren't for you, I wouldn't be here now. I can't thank you enough for all that you have done for me, I am in your debt."

Barry asked Michelle for Lucas's mobile number and if he could borrow her car as his car had been sold whilst he was in prison. Barry was going to do his usual trick and track Lucas down by his phone. She gave him Lucas's number and her car keys as she trusted Barry to bring Lucas back. Barry finished his tea and was about to head for the door, but before he left, Michelle told him that he was welcome to stay around hers for a couple of weeks until he could get back on his feet, as he had lost his house after being in prison.

As Barry opened the front door, he looked at Michelle and said to her, "Thank you, Michelle, but I don't think it's going to look very good for you having a criminal staying in your house. I'll find myself an apartment to stay in." Barry went into Michelle's car and tracked Lucas down on his phone.

Barry rang Lucas's phone and found a trace of him in Chelsea, so he stepped on the pedal and headed there as quickly as possible. After an hour's drive, he got to Chelsea and followed the directions to where Lucas appeared to be on the phone. He drove around at the location and could see that he was getting nearer and nearer but still couldn't see any signs of Lucas.

Barry drove around the road near Chelsea common, where his phone showed him the place Lucas currently was at. Barry thought of getting out of the vehicle and having a look around for him. Until then, he heard a guy shouting just further down the road and mentioning Lucas's name. It sounded like a threat, so Barry followed the destination where he heard a voice come from and turned right down S Parade Road, where he saw a young man running towards him, panicking like if he was being chased.

Barry didn't even notice the guy but as he watched the guy run, he saw a gang of thugs on his tail chasing him down Chelsea square.

"You can't run from us, Lucas, you've got nowhere to go, it's time for you to pay!" they said, and just then after hearing the guy shout, Barry noticed that the man being chased was Lucas.

Barry followed the chase in his car and kept a close eye on Lucas. He could see that Lucas was running out of energy and it wasn't taking long for the gang to catch him up, he had to do something fast. He pulled over as close as he could to Lucas and opened the door; he shouted, "Lucas! Quick, get in!"

The first thing Lucas thought was who this strange man was asking him to get into the car, and if he could trust him. But with seconds until he was about to get caught, Lucas felt that he had no choice but to trust the man and get into the car as it was the only choice he had. He got into the vehicle and Barry stepped on it, taking Lucas safely back home to Sidcup. As Barry took Lucas home, he started to have a discussion with him as he tried to wonder what was going on.

Barry – "That seemed like quite a mean lot you were with back there; do you want to talk about it? You know if this is meant to be some sort of game Lucas, it doesn't look very friendly."

Lucas – "How do you know my name?"

Barry – "I met you when you were a child."

Lucas – "Well, I've never seen you before, in my whole life. Who are you?"

Barry – "Like I said, I met you when you were a baby, so you won't recognise me. I'm Barry Dermative. I'm a friend of your mothers'."

Lucas – "Ah… So you're the man who mum's been talking about, the great detective."

Barry – "Why were those guys after you?"

Lucas – "Like you said, it was just a game."

Barry then looked below Lucas' legs and spotted a bag he was carrying. He asked Lucas what he had inside but

Lucas said nothing. He started getting fed up of Barry's questions and started getting the attitude.

"You know what man, shut up! Just shut up! This is all you coppers do, isn't it? Questions, questions!" Lucas shouted.

Barry then quickly pulled over the car and looked at Lucas in the eye as he told him straight that he was not tolerating nonsense.

"Now you listen here, young man, I didn't just come here to clean up your mess. I didn't come here just to listen to your gob, I could go home and enjoy a nice hot cup of tea. But no, I'm stuck here cleaning your crap! Whatever the situation you're in is, I'm the only one who can save you. The police want evidence and have you got any?"

Lucas just shook his head at Barry and his face dropped as he could tell that Barry was right. "I didn't think so and if you go back out there, you'll be killed."

After having a little clash, Lucas started to talk to Barry to try and get to know him better.

Lucas – "So, you were a copper once?"

Barry – "Used to be, yes."

Lucas – "Did you retire from it?"

Barry – "Retire? Ha! I'd still be there if I could, kicking bad guy's ass. Yeah, I used to love doing that job. I wish I could have it back, but I can't complain, it was my fault. I shouldn't have been such an idiot like I was. If hadn't had made such a foolish mistake, I wouldn't have lost my dream job."

Lucas asked Barry about what happened, but before Barry would say anything to him, he told him not to mention anything about it to anyone. Lucas promised Barry from his heart that he would not say a word to anyone, and Barry knew deep down that he could trust Lucas as he was the son of his best friend Michelle. He told him all about his past when he was a copper and what he did wrong to lose his career.

Barry – "When I was a police officer, I worked undercover as a detective. I absolutely loved the job and I never stopped working although I didn't earn much. I only earned £800 a month for the job, which was £9200 a year. At first, it didn't really bother me how much I earnt, cause I just loved doing the job. But then, you realise after a while that it was actually a decent sum of money to earn, but it still wasn't enough for a living wage."

Barry – "The more money I earned the more I had to pay on taxes. It's the same on anything you do, the more you earn more you pay back to the government. You only earn half what it says on your wage."

Barry – "Once I was on a chase scene, and I caught one of the biggest drug criminals in the UK. The first thing he asked me when I caught him was how much I earned for just going around chasing criminals like him. He told me he earned twenty grand or more just for breaking the law on drugs, but that wasn't all he said. He kept telling me that, the law was robbing us, using us as slaves. And when I watched the bills come through my letter box, I just suddenly felt like as if I believed him."

Barry – "So then, I made a bargain with him whilst he was in the cells and made a deal with him that I'd get him out by swapping the bag of cocaine for a bag of plain flour. He promised me for his freedom he'd give me some of the money, which he did, but not much. Instead, he got me in his gang of smugglers, where I earnt a fortune for myself."

Barry – "But it was only a month until my own police colleagues realised what I was up to and they searched my property. They found the drugs I was taking, and then I was arrested, sentenced to 17 years in prison. Now I realise, it might make you feel good, a man on top of the world. The money, the drugs, all of it. But as soon as you cross that line, you are at the stage where you could also lose everything, your house, family, money, even your life!"

After hearing Barry explain his story, Lucas felt a certain bond of friendship, and felt that he could trust him. He thought that it was only fair to tell Barry his problem after hearing his, as he thought maybe Barry could help him.

"I've got a daughter called Lyla, she's one-year-old today. I've sent a birthday card and a present to my girlfriend's house," Lucas said.

Barry asked Lucas why he wasn't at his girlfriend's house going to see his daughter, he offered to give Lucas a lift but Lucas refused to go. He asked him why he wouldn't go to see his daughter as he started to have the feeling that there was something Lucas was hiding. But then, Lucas gave Barry the bag that he had and when Barry looked inside, he could clearly see that there were drugs inside.

"What's this? Cocaine?" Barry asked, and Lucas told him that it wasn't cocaine it was actually bags of mephedrone.

Barry was shocked, and he started raising his voice, as he knew what the situation was like when getting into drugs.

"What the hell are you doing with this? Where'd you get this from? Did those men give this to you?" he asked, and Lucas explained to him how he ended up with the drugs.

Lucas – "I have been hanging about with them for a while now, about a month or so. I never really had many friends, I don't know what it was people saw in me but I just never met anyone really at school. I was quiet and all on my own. It got boring after a while. Suddenly, one day on my way back, I met these lads down the alley. They just said 'hello' to me and they welcomed me in the brotherhood. I never realised what they really were doing until the first time they gave me the drugs."

Lucas – "I always said to my mum that I'd never get involved in anything like drugs and I meant it. If I'd have known who they were at the time I would never had got involved. They kept persuading me to smoke the drugs, saying how good it was, how it'll make me feel good. So I took a small puff to please them but I hated it, it was awful. Now they keep giving bags full of drugs wanting me to pay money that I can't afford."

Barry – "How much are they asking from you for the drugs?"

Lucas – "They want to sell them for no less than twenty-five grand. If I don't, they'll get me to buy it from them for thirty-five grand, ten grand more than the price for me selling them."
  Barry told Lucas that those guys won't stop until they have their money. They would do whatever it took them to get their money off of Lucas, even if it took them to harm a close member of his family. Lucas straightaway started to worry as he didn't want anything to happen to his mum, especially that would end up being his responsibility. He asked Barry what he was supposed to do, but Barry didn't know as Lucas had really put himself in an awkward spot. If Lucas went to the police, he could get done for committing a crime and if he goes back, he would be killed. But just then, Lucas thought of an idea, he said to Barry, "You can help me!" Barry wondered why Lucas would say that. But Lucas knew that Barry didn't come here for no reason.

Lucas – "You said it yourself, Barry, you didn't just come here for no reason. You are doing this for my mother, aren't you? Also, like you said you're, the only person who can get me out of this. You miss all the action, chasing down baddies. Well now's your one chance to do it again, be a hero, redeem yourself for your mistakes."

Barry – "Yes, that's a good point, I never thought of it like that. Alright yes I'll help you, but on three conditions. Number one: I lead. Number two: you listen to everything I say at all times, and Number three: you never disobey me at any cost whatsoever, if you do, you're on your own!"

Lucas told Barry that he understood the three rules he was given, and so then Barry agreed to help. But before he took Lucas, home he headed straight down the road towards the Albert Bridge as he needed Lucas to get rid of the drugs. "Where are we going?" Lucas asked.

Barry said to him, "There's something you've got to do first before you go home."

Barry got to Chelsea Embankment road and parked the car on the side of the road by the river. As he stopped the vehicle, he pointed at the river and told Lucas to dump the drugs. But Lucas thought Barry was out of his mind, he found that a ridiculous idea as he felt that he was sure to get caught for throwing stuff in the Thames.

"Are you nuts? I can't do that. I can't just throw drugs in the Thames, there's probably camera's out there!" But then Barry reminded him about disobeying him as Lucas was already breaking the three rules.

Barry – "Ah! Already starting, disobeying me. Remember what I said about the three rules."

Lucas – "Alright, alright! I'll do it."

Lucas got out of the car with the bag and quickly headed to the river. He opened the bag and threw the whole lot into the Thames before heading straight back to the car. Lucas got back in the vehicle and asked Barry what was going to happen next. Barry told him that he was going to make sure that these guys never bothered him again.

"I thought you were going to take me home?" Lucas asked, and Barry told him that he would, but first. he needed to find out more about what Lucas had got himself into if he was to help him get out.

Barry asked Lucas if he knew who the leader of this drug gang was so that he could find out more on what he was up against, and Barry wasn't surprised when he heard Lucas's response.

"I've never met the leader of the gang; I've spoken to him on the phone once but never seen him face to face. They all say he's the one man that you don't want to mess with, the most dangerous man in the UK. You even say his name and your life is in harm. Loki!"

Barry – "Loki?"

Lucas – "What? Do you know him?"

Barry – "Do I know him? He was the criminal that I released from the cell and made a deal with. It's because of me that you are in this situation. It's because of me that low life is out there causing havoc to our society. He took me for a fool, made me look like a prat, left me to rot in those cells while he was out there doing his dirty work. Now, it's time for him to pay for what he's done; to me, to the police, and to the public. It's time for him to see how it feels to rot away like a piece of meat"

Lucas – "What're you going to do?"

Barry – "I'm going to hunt that piece of filth down, and I'm going to kill him!"

Barry asked Lucas for his phone and Barry looked at Lucas' contacts. Barry could see some threating texts that Lucas had received from a person called Verne, so then without asking Lucas, he just sent a message to Verne as he was planning a meeting. Lucas asked Barry what he was doing, and all Barry said was, "We're having a welcome party!"

He told Verne to meet him tomorrow night at the Greenwich Park to come and collect his money at midnight. Lucas was getting concerned as he wasn't sure Barry actually knew what he was getting himself into.

"Do you know who these guys are? They won't answer. They answer to no one," Lucas said, but Barry knew that all they wanted was money and as long as he had money they wouldn't refuse.

Barry received a text back from Verne saying that he accepted the arrangement and was willing to meet them tomorrow evening. Barry took Lucas home and told him not to mention anything to his mum about what was going on, they were best to keep it between themselves. He parked the car back on drive way and they both approached the door. Lucas rang the doorbell and when Michelle answered the door, she was so happy to see that he was safe and she thanked Barry for bringing him back.

Barry gave Michelle back her car keys and said goodbye as he was about to head off to his apartment, but Michelle asked him if he was sure he didn't want to stay the night as it was a very long way for him to walk in a cold dark night. Barry still refused to stay as he didn't feel it would be right for her. Then she told him that if he wouldn't stay then the least she could do was offer him a lift and so she gave him a ride in the car to his apartment whilst Lucas stayed in the house.

Michelle dropped Barry off to his hotel at the Travelodge in Sidcup, where he was currently staying. It was only a 30 minutes' drive from her house, and when she arrived at the place, she had one question to ask Barry: "How did you find him so quickly? It's like you knew where he was. Please, Barry, tell me is he in trouble?"

But Barry didn't feel comfortable telling Michelle about the situation Lucas had got himself into because he didn't want her to worry.

He said to Michelle, "He just got into the wrong crowd of people, he knows now who not to hang about with, you have got nothing to worry about." Barry left the vehicle and entered the property; he collected his keys from the reception and went to his room.

The following morning, Barry went to the local bank and drew out £15,000 in cash. He put the money in an envelope and quickly headed back to his hotel as he was waiting for a car to arrive that he was going to rent. Barry was renting a Suzuki Reno 2006, and the car arrived at the hotel at 9 o'clock in the morning. The man gave Barry a form to sign before giving him the keys to the vehicle. At 10 pm,

Barry got himself dressed and put the money in his briefcase, getting ready to go to Michelle's. He locked the door and gave his keys to the receptionist before stepping in to his new vehicle.

He drove up the road to Michelle's house and knocked on the door for Lucas. The first moment when Michelle opened the door, she and Lucas both spotted Barry's new car that he was renting.

"Nice car, did you get that from the scrap yard?" Lucas said. Michelle told Lucas not to be so rude. Barry didn't have much time to chat, so he got Lucas in the car and headed to the Greenwich Park.

When they got to the park, they waited for Verne to arrive at the scene; until they saw a group of men appear in the fields in front of them. Lucas got a call on the phone from Verne telling him that he had arrived. He told him that he was on his way before he put the phone down and waited in the car with Barry.

"That's them! Why are we sitting here? They're already out there waiting for us," Lucas asked Barry, but Barry had a plan, he was just waiting for the exact moment. He knew that if Lucas didn't show up, then they would split up to search for him, and Barry's plan was working as after ten minutes Verne was started to react as he felt he was being tricked.

"Show yourself, Lucas. You think you can play games with us? You're making a big mistake!" he shouted. Verne split up with his two colleagues, Sye and Monty, holding their guns in their hands, hunting for Lucas as they were going to kill him.

Barry watched the guys split up and straightaway he knew his plan was working. "It's time for action!" he said, as he got out of the car with the case and told Lucas to stay in the vehicle. Barry sneaked through the park carefully to find the men hunting for Lucas; he picked up a plastic supermarket bag left on the field and carried it with him on the way.

Barry saw one of the guys straight in front of him and coming in his direction, so he quickly hid behind the tree and got the bag open in his hands. He waited behind the trees as silent as he could until the man went past. He watched Sye go past and quickly went in for the attack, approaching him from behind and putting the bag on his head using all his strength to suffocate him. When Sye was out cold, Barry took his gun and dragged his body into the bush so that Monty and Verne wouldn't notice.

Barry saw Monty heading towards the Roman Temple and he followed him on his tail. Barry could then see that Monty was walking around the building so he had an idea. He went to the corner of the building where he saw Monty going and at the moment he had him cornered. When Barry got close enough, he sneaked behind Monty and knocked him out with the gun on the back of his head. Now there was only Verne left.

Verne walked across the field and started to feel concerned as he couldn't see any signs of Sye or Monty. He shouted for them

"Sye! Monty! Where are you?" Until then, he got a strange response.

"You're wasting your breath shouting for them, cause they're not showing up."

Barry walked towards Verne with his briefcase in his hand and the gun in his jacket pocket.

"Who the hell are you?" Verne asked Barry, holding his gun straight at him.

Barry – "Never mind who I am, I want to make a deal."

Verne – "That depends on what?"

Barry – "In this case is £15,000. This ends now! Take this and walk away and swear that you'll never go near the boy again."

Verne – "And if we refuse?"

Barry – "Then you'll end up like your friends"

Verne – "That's very tempting, but I'm afraid the offer is too low. So, unless you've got any more money to add I suggest you wave your day's goodbye. You killed my guys so you will die with them."

Barry then tricked Verne as he tried to look in his pocket for more cash.

"Here hold this!" Barry said, throwing the brief case at Verne making his drop his gun on the floor. As Verne caught the case Barry forced the gun out of his pocket and quickly shot the gun at the briefcase making the bullet go right through and into Verne. Barry picked up his briefcase and also took Verne's mobile phone.

He looked at Verne on the ground and said to him, "You should've taken my offer!" He got back into the car and Lucas started having a go as he had just seen what he had done to Verne.

"You killed him, you actually killed him!"

Barry – "They were going to kill you, I had no choice. There are loads more of them out there after you. So before you say anything, just think about the situation you've put yourself in!"

Barry looked at Verne's phone to see if he could find any text or any signs of locations on where these gangs were hanging about as he knew that the more he found these gangs, the more he'd find Loki.

"You took a phone from them?" Lucas asked.

And Barry told him, "Dealers have a location spot where they like to hang about and arrange their plots. That's why with every phone I collect from these men, the more info I can find by these messages on where all of them are based. The more info I get from them the closer I get to finding Loki!"

Just then, Barry found a text to a man called Zacos which also gave him the address to his property. Barry drove Lucas home and went to pay Zacos a visit. He found the address on his phone and when he approached the building, he knocked on the door to see if he was at home. When Zacos answered the door, Barry could straightaway see that Zacos was strapped to an oxygen tank, but that was not going to make him stop at anything in getting the information that he needed for him.

Barry introduced himself as a health insurance man and spoke to Zacos about his health cost.

"Good evening, sir, you must be Zacos, lovely property you have here I must say. I'm here to talk about the cover of your health insurance."

Zacos had been another member of the drug gang years ago until he had realised what he had got himself into and he tried to forfeit his way out.

When Zacos told the gang straight that he had enough of it all, they weren't going to let him go without charge, so they told him to pay up. They told him to pay £20,000 in cash straightaway or die. But Zacos had nothing with him and they shot him there on the spot leaving him to rot on the street.

He laid there bleeding out. He was sure that he was going to die, but fortunately, he was found and taken to the hospital on time. The bullet hit Zacos on the left side of his body and damaged his lung. Now Zacos had only one lung working properly and had to breathe through an oxygen tube on an oxygen tank to survive.

Zacos tried to tell Barry that he didn't need any health insurance but nothing was going to stop Barry from getting answers. Barry stepped into the property and got him to sit down on the chair. Barry went over to the oxygen tank said to Zacos, "You know you said 'you don't need health insurance', well I can assure you, you're going to need it when I'm done with you!" He turned the machine on full blast causing all the oxygen to go so strong in Zacos, making him struggle to breath. After a few seconds, Barry turned the machine back down, and with the oxygen so strong it caused Zacos to cough.

As Zacos was coughing, trying to get his breath back, he said to Barry, "What the hell is your problem?"

Barry kept forcing him to talk and he tried to play a hard game on refusing but didn't win as Barry kept turning the machine up just making him choke even more and more.

Eventually, after Barry had turned the machine up three times, Zacos chocked his words out, and decided to talk. Barry asked him why his number and address was on Verne's phone, he knew that there could only be one reason for that, and that was for him working with them. He asked Zacos to explain why he was in this drug smuggling gang and more importantly where Loki was. But Zacos told Barry that he was getting the total wrong end of the stick, he did not have anything to do with these drug-dealing criminals and didn't know where Loki was.

Barry didn't believe a word that came out of Zacos' mouth; he went to the oxygen tank and was about to turn the switch up again. Zacos watched Barry and as he saw him about to turn the machine he shouted, trying to tell Barry that this was no joke, "No, No, No! Wait it's true. I haven't seen him, honestly. I used to be part of his gang years ago, that I'm not proud of. But since then I haven't seen him, or any of them."

So then Barry asked Zacos, "If that's true, and you haven't seen him or been working for him, then why is your number and address on this phone that belongs to one of his dealers?" Zacos explained to Barry that the reason why they had his details was that those dealers were after him, and they wanted him dead.

Zacos – "Oh, those low life scums have been after me ever since I left the gang. Anyone who leaves the gang is dead to them; as long as they have their money, they don't care what or who you are! If you refuse to pay the money or refuse to sell the drugs, they will finish you anyway, and this is a proof example!"

Barry – "He shot you, didn't he? Loki shot you?"

Zacos told Barry that if he wasn't stuck breathing through the earth on his machine, he would teach Loki a lesson for what he did to him, and after hearing that, Barry stepped in. He told Zacos that he was not the only person whose life

Loki had ruined, he had ruined his as well, and now Loki was on the edge of ruining the life of a young teenager who Barry was trying to save. Barry was aiming to finish this once and for all as he wanted Loki dead, and by the look of the eyes of Zacos, he could tell that he did as well.

But Zacos still didn't have a clue where Loki was. He knew he used to see him hang about by the Piccadilly underground, but that was years ago. However, Zacos did know someone who could be of more use to Barry on helping him find Loki, but Barry was going to need to be very clever on getting sense into this man if he was to get anything out of him.

Pavilo Derang was an old friend of Zacos and another guy who had got himself involved in the gang of smugglers because they offered him a lot of money if he'd help. At that time, he was homeless and living on the streets. Pavilo was a sweet kind man who had been taught to love; he was not a man that could hurt anyone. But one day it all changed as Pavilo didn't realise what a bunch of animals he had got involved with. Pavilo got them their money like they said each time, but would refuse to lay a finger on anyone. These cold-hearted criminals couldn't accept a soft-hearted man on their turf so they forced him to change his habit on being soft by grabbing an innocent young woman in front of him. They gave him a gun and whilst another was aimed at his head they told Pavilo that it was time to change.

They told him to shoot the woman down and warned him that if he refused, he wouldn't get the money he wanted; he would be killed himself before the woman. Pavilo just felt terrified, he was too scared to die so he felt he had no choice but to do it. He picked up the gun and closed his eyes and he pulled the trigger at the girl. Now, ever since then, Pavilo's life has been destroyed. After he came out of prison, he has felt nothing but deep sorrow and guilt. Pavilo kept wishing to god that he could bring back the girl and take him instead; he wished he had never let them make him kill the girl.

So, Pavilo goes to the White Horse pub at Piccadilly Circus every afternoon drinking shots of rum, until he gets wasted to the end. He feels that this is the only thing that makes him feel better, draining his sorrows and his guilt, and he now feels he has no life left in him. Zacos, in his recent times, had tried speaking to him but he just would not listen, he wouldn't listen to anybody. Zacos told Barry that if he really could get Pavilo to get some sense and get him to talk, then he would be the man to help him find Loki.

Barry headed for the door and thanked Zacos for his help. As he left the room, he told Zacos in a promise, "I will find him, this will end soon. No more hiding in fear, no more sitting in the dark, this ends now. You have my word."

Barry left the flat and drove straight over to the White Horse pub, he parked his car in the car park glanced at the building. As Barry first entered the door, he saw a man sat at the bar on a stall wearing a fur coat. He saw the guy ordering 4 shots of whiskey and downing them like a glass of water.

Barry said to himself, "There's only one guy who could be downing that many shots so fast."

Barry went to the bar and sat on the stall next to the man. He ordered two shots and told the bartender to make this Pavilo's last. But Pavilo was already on the edge on getting drunk and wasn't amused with Barry making decisions for him as he didn't even know who the hell he was.

"Who the hell do you think you are coming here giving orders? Who gave you the right to decide what I can or cannot do?" Pavilo said in a drunken manner and Barry told him that he needed to have a little chat with him about something, and told him that just sitting here drinking himself away wasn't going to get him anywhere. Barry raised his glass to Pavilo and downed the shots together. They sat at the bar and Barry started to talk to him to try and get him to understand the right way forward. He told him that he knew why he was doing this but Pavilo didn't believe a word that he said.

Barry – "I know why you're doing this but this isn't helping you. Drinking your sorrows out to ease the pain. It's just going to make you feel worse again."

Pavilo – "You know nothing! You don't have a clue what's happened in my life."

Barry – "Really? OK then I'll tell you everything that I do know, and you tell me what it is that I don't. I know that you used to live on the streets; I know that you joined a group of dealers because they offered to give you money to help you get off the streets. I know that the reason you are sitting here right now drinking shots every day is because you've shot cold an innocent young woman and now, ever since you pulled that trigger, you feel not just guilt but ashamed that you let your fear of death stand in the way. You now feel you should've taken your own life and not hers."

Pavilo couldn't believe that Barry knew so much, it was like he had read his mind. He asked him how he knew so much and Barry told him that he had just seen an old friend of his who Pavilo knew well. He told Pavilo what situation Zacos was in and that now thanks to these low life drug gangs who shot him, he has to breathe through oxygen using an oxygen tank and tube for the rest of his life.

"There is a boy who I'm trying to save, he has got himself involved in this as well. And if this isn't stopped soon, he could end up like us. Now we can end all this, get justice for you, for me, for Zacos, and for the boy. All I need you to do is tell me where Loki is." Barry asked Pavilo.

Pavilo – "You think you can defeat Loki on your own? You must be joking. He has men everywhere; you go out there it'll be suicide!"

Barry – "I know! Which is why I won't be going alone. What you did wasn't your fault, they forced you to do it and if you come and help me now, you will save hell of a lot more lives from being ruined, if you just tell me where he is?"

Pavilo told him that Loki was at the EKE night club. This was where Loki and his gang met up at night for dealing more drugs to the community. He told Barry that Loki was usually in the office of the building upstairs but was guarded by his assistants. No one was allowed in there without permission unless they were there to sell drugs.

Barry then had a plan. He told Pavilo that it was time to pay Loki a visit, but Pavilo thought he was out of his mind.

"Are you crazy? Did you not listen to a word that I just said? They won't let you in there. As soon as you appear at that door and they notice who you are, you'll be dead." Pavilo said.

But Barry told him not to worry as he had a plan and was confident that they were going to let him in as long as he had a hand full of drugs. He headed for the exit and told Pavilo that he'd be waiting for five minutes for him to make his decision on whether or not he was coming and if not, Barry was going alone.

Pavilo sat there staring at the shot glass feeling ashamed of himself; he knew nothing was going to change what he had done. However, deep inside, he knew that this could be the moment where he could redeem himself. So then, he ran out of the door and went with Barry.

When they got in the car, Pavilo directed Barry to the EKE night club and when they got there, Barry could clearly see that it was crowded with dealers. Pavilo was more and more panicking and was starting to think that Barry was leading them to suicide.

"I don't know what it is you have in mind, but whatever it is, it's suicide! You'll never be able to get past all them lot," he said.

Barry told Pavilo not to worry so much, as he knew how to handle these dealers. Barry saw one of the guys approaching and got out of the car to show Pavilo how it's done. He could see that the guy was trying to have a cigarette but didn't have a lighter so Barry offered him his. He lit the guy's cigarette and as soon as the guy had his head down, Barry knocked him out unconscious.

Barry quickly checked the guy's pockets before anyone else came. He grabbed his phone and his bag of cocaine before he got back to the car. He told Pavilo that he was going inside the building and that he needed him to go with him, so then they both entered the club and were headed for the office upstairs. But it wasn't very long until they were caught by one of the dealers. Lloyd spotted Barry and Pavilo walking towards the stairs and he knew they were nothing to do with the gang. He stopped them from trespassing and asked them what they were doing in the building.

"Hey you two, what the hell are you doing here?"

Barry showed Lloyd the bag of drugs that he had and told him that they had come to see Loki and make a deal with him. Lloyd took the two men up to the office to see Loki and told him that they were here to make a deal. Loki looked at Barry and asked him who he was, but straightaway Barry could see that the man wasn't actually Loki. The man impersonating Loki was actually a guy called Herman Noah, one of Loki's closest allies in the community. Barry introduced himself to Herman and told him that he had come to make a deal as he showed him his bag of cocaine and told him that he had lots of it. Herman opened the bag of coke and tested it to see if it was real. He sniffed the drug and when he found out that it was actually cocaine, he told Barry to bring the whole lot. So then Barry headed outside and opened the boot of the car where he had five huge white bags filled with white powder.

Barry and Pavilo took the bags upstairs in the office to Herman, and straightaway Barry asked Herman, "So how much you going to pay me for this?"

Herman gave Barry £30,000 for the drugs and told him to clear off before he changed his mind and killed him

Barry told Pavilo to wait inside the car whilst he just had a cigarette outside. He walked through the back and could see through the window, two of the dealers carrying the bags into the storeroom. He hid behind the wall so they couldn't see him and waited for them to leave. As soon as all the bags were taken into the storeroom, Barry looked in the room and could see that the whole room was just filled with drugs.

"Say goodbye to your trash!" he said as he grabbed his cigarette and threw it towards the bags of white powder. He ran back to the car and got in as quickly as possible, driving away from the building before the building blew up.

The moment Barry drove off; the building blew up like a bomb. All the glass from the windows went everywhere and parts from the building fell onto the ground. Rest of the building was just nothing but flames. Pavilo heard a massive bang coming from behind him and when he saw the building on fire, he was shell shocked.

"What did you just do?" he shouted, and Barry told him that the bags were actually filled with potassium chlorate.

"You killed him, you killed Loki" Pavilo said, but then Barry told him that they had been tricked as that wasn't the real Loki.

"That man was not Loki! That man pretending to be him was Herman Noah, one of Loki's closest allies. Now I don't know what their game is here, but I will never forget the face of that man. And I will know him when I see him!" When Barry looked at the man's pass, he could see that the guy he had knocked out was called Luis Coleman. He used Coleman's phone to call Herman's number and just as Barry suspected Loki picked up the phone.

Loki – "You better have a good reason for calling me, Coleman!"

Barry – "Hello, Loki, do you remember me?"

Loki – "Who the hell is this? Where's Coleman?"

Barry – "Coleman is dead, and so are all your other pig heads in the EKE. Oh and even more good news for you, your EKE club is destroyed."

Loki – "You better start explaining; otherwise, you'll be putting your name down on the funeral list!"

63

Barry – "I don't think so. You have ruined so many lives including mine. You might not remember me, but I could never forget you. I am going to take back what you stole from me and all those other innocent people. I'm coming for you Loki!" Barry put the phone down and straightaway tracked Herman's phone that Loki was using. He found a location on Loki at the Old Quevo night club, which was abandoned years ago. As Barry started the engine of the vehicle ready to be on his way to the Quevo, his own mobile rang, and when Barry looked, he could see it was Michelle, so Barry turned the engine off and answered.

Michelle told Barry that she was concerned about Lucas as since the day Barry bought him home Lucas had now disappeared again. She told Barry that she heard Lucas mention the name Loki and that raised a concern on Barry as he now knew that Lucas was in more trouble than he had hoped. He told Michelle that he'll find Lucas and find out what is going on. When he put the phone down, he headed for the Quevo club.

Meanwhile, at the Quevo club, Loki was getting really agitated as someone was after him.

"Some lunatic is trying to destroy our business. He killed half our men and destroyed the EKE club. Are you going to allow him to cause any more damage?" Loki shouted to his men. He told six of his guys named Luke, Wayne, Mitchell, Phillip, Cliff, and Nike to stay behind and wait for Barry to approach so that when he does, they would ambush him and kill him.

Loki had Lucas at the Quevo with him Lucas was Loki's messenger boy telling everything on where Barry was and what he was up too. Lucas was only doing what Loki told him to do for his own sake and for the money Loki kept giving him. Lucas was too scared to refuse as he knew how smart Loki was, there was nowhere to hide or run, because Loki knew every bit of detail about Lucas and would find him like a flash as he had men everywhere. Lucas knew that if he refused then he would be killed. However, Lucas didn't know that by telling Loki info he was setting Barry up.

As Loki was about to leave the property, Lucas told him that Barry was on his way but Loki didn't recognise who Lucas was on about. So then, Lucas mentioned the word ex-cop and that straightaway flashed a memory in Loki's mind, and he finally realised who Lucas was talking about.

"Ah… So the great old detective is on his way is he? He's more of a loser than I thought."

At that moment, Loki had a plan on how to get Barry. He went over to the guys and told Nike, Luke, Wayne, Phillip, Cliff and Mitchell to go and pay the boys mum a visit at her house and keep her company. Lucas reacted as he didn't want anything to happen to his mum.

Lucas – "This wasn't part of the agreement, my mum's nothing to do with this. Leave her alone!"

Loki – "Oh but she is, boy. You see, you failed to get me my money, I sent some of my guys out to make an agreement with you but still, you let me down, and whenever people do that, the price is blood! When I say blood, I mean from the heart. Someone that it will really hurt to lose, so that next time, boy, you won't let me down!"

Lucas lost it. He ran up to Loki as he shouted threats towards him, but then Loki grabbed hold of Lucas by the neck and held a knife in his hand.

"Don't test me, boy! Now you see what it's like trying to mess with me? If you still love her that much maybe I can do you a favour later on and put you out of your misery," he said.

Loki got his mobile out and quickly called Barry. Barry heard his phone ring and quickly pulled over to stop the vehicle and answered the phone. When Barry was on the phone, Loki straightaway started to torment him as he asked him how he felt being let out after seventeen years. Barry asked Loki how he knew it was him on the line. But then, Barry was up for a shock.

Loki – "I've got a young friend of yours, telling me everything that I need to know about you, Barry; where you live, where you are and even what you're up too. In other words, this young man here tells me everything I need to know just to set you up and make your life a misery."

Loki passed the phone over to Lucas and told him to say hello to Barry. When Barry heard Lucas on the phone, he straightaway started to worry as he knew that Lucas was in danger.

"Lucas! What're you doing? Loki I swear if you lay a finger on the boy I'll...!"

While Barry was raising his voice on the phone Loki held the phone towards the ground and laughed. He found it so amusing listening to Barry's threats. He waited until Barry had finished his reaction, and then told him that he was wasting his time.

Loki – "Have you finished wasting your breath? Why would I want to kill him now after all the hard work he's done? You see, Barry, thanks to this boy. He's the reason you're here. He tells me everything just for a small amount of cash. After he's been with you, he goes home and he simply runs back to me and tells me everything, and when he does that I give him £500 in cash. The truth hurts, doesn't it Barry? Not just has he messed your life up, but he's also messed his mother's as well."

Barry – "Michelle? What has she got to do with this?"

Loki – "Well, it's quite simple, Barry. You see, although Lucas maybe my right-hand messenger, the question is, do I really need him? No! He's let me down Barry, failed to deliver business, and even failed to pay up because of that. When people do that to me, the penalty for it is blood. Usually, we take blood from relatives just so the suspect can see what it's like to be let down but now that you're on the way, I'll leave you to decide the fate. I've got the boy here at the Quevo club which I should imagine is where you're headed now. But also going to the boy's house are six of my men to pay your lovely friend a visit. So! Who you going to save, Barry? The

66

boy or his mum? One life is ours to take and one is yours to save. Choose well!"

Loki put the phone down and Barry was starting to panic badly as he realised that not just had Lucas put his own life at stake but his mother's as well. Barry knew he was not going to get to the house in time before the men did so he thought that he had only one option; to call the police.

"What're you doing?" Pavilo asked, and Barry explained the situation and told him that he had to call the police. He dialled the emergency number on his mobile and got through to the London Police Department. He spoke to his old friend Glen who was not amused to hear Barry again.

Sargent Collins – "This is Sargent Collins, Chief of the London Police Department, how can I help?"

Barry – "Hey Glen! It's me, Barry!"

Sargent Collins – "Barry! You've got some nerve to be calling us. What do you want from us? What is it? More debt, more drugs?"

Barry – "Don't start Collins all that's in the past, I've changed. I admit to what I did, I know I messed up and for that I'm sorry."

Sargent Collins – "You can say that again! Do you know how much trouble you caused to this police department? We almost had to close this force down because of you!"

Barry – "I'm truly sorry about that, but please listen."

Sargent Collins – "Why should I, Barry, hey? Tell me why should I? What's it going to be more lies, more excuses?"

Barry – "Will you just listen to me? This is not a lie, this is not an excuse! There is a group of men going to a house to attack an innocent young woman. The house is 23 Brexton

Street in Sidcup. If you have the guts to be who you say you are then at least have the decency to send your troops out to help her!!"

When Glen put the phone down, he could tell by Barry's reaction on the other side of the line that he was not kidding, and he knew that although he might have made some bad mistakes the one thing that Barry never did was lie, he was always honest. He got out of his office and straightaway called the scene, getting as many of his men out as he could.

Back in the car, Pavilo asked Barry if he was confident that the police would help, but Barry knew that it was their job to help people and that Glen was a good man he could trust. He drove to the Quevo night club as he told Pavilo: "We've got one life to save and one life to kill!"

They got to the Quevo club and entered the building. Loki noticed Barry had come in the building and he said to him, "So, I see you decided to save the boy, I must say what a shame it is for the boy's mother, so innocent and yet has to suffer!"

Barry saw Loki approaching holding Lucas hostage with a knife at his throat. He just shook his head with the look of despair and said to Loki, "You find all this so amusing don't you; ruining innocent lives, killing people? This is like a big game to you, isn't it? It's time for you to pay Loki, for everything. The lives you've taken, the families you've ruined. It's time for you to die!"

Loki – "Yeah well maybe your right Barry, maybe I do deserve to die, but let's not be too hasty shall we? As you can see here, I have the boy and my men are armed. I think there's been enough blood shared for one day, so I'm allowing you to take the boy and go. However, if you try and cause any disturbance, Barry, then I'll kill the boy and you'd have caused more blood spill on my hands."

Barry knew that he had no choice but to agree, as Lucas would be killed and most likely so would he and Pavilo. He nodded his head and agreed to the take the boy and leave without harm. When Loki let Lucas go, he headed out the door with Barry and Pavilo, but Barry knew he wasn't finished with Loki yet. He walked out the door and stared at him as he said to him that this wasn't over.

Wayne and his gang got to Michelle's house and knocked on her door leaving their weapons in their pockets. She answered the door and could see six men in hooded jackets and jumpers, all had their hoods up and their mouths covered with scarves.

"Good afternoon Ms, we just thought you might like some company, may we come in?" Wayne asked, and straight away Michelle was in shock, she could tell that this was trouble.

She spoke kindly and truthfully to the guys telling them that's she was fine on her own as she closed the door. But Wayne knew that it wasn't going to work being easy so then he went in hard.

He stopped her from closing the door as he pushed it open and said to her, "Now that's just rude, I think it's time we taught you some manners!" Wayne entered the house as he grabbed Michelle by the hair and went to the kitchen. Nike and Luke went inside the house with him whilst Cliff, Phillip and Mitchell stayed outside for look out. Michelle started crying, asking the men what they wanted, but all the guys did was torment her and smashed up her house for fun.

A few seconds later the police arrived. Cliff, Phillip and Mitchell saw two police cars at the scene; they straightaway got their guns out and fired at the vehicles. When their guns ran out of ammo, they quickly took cover and the police got out of their vehicles before the gun fight began. Detective Carl was on the scene with PC Derek, PC Griffin and PC Goodman, and when the shooting began it wasn't long until Carl had shot down Cliff.

Wayne heard the shooting outside and wondered what the hell was going on. He called Phillip on his phone asking him what was going on and Phillip told him that it was the police. Wayne was pissed off and thought Michelle had called the police, he got out his gun and held it at her head.

"Did you call the cops?" he asked her, and Michelle said to him, "No! I didn't even know they were here!"

Then the police cleared the entrance and made their way into the house. The police didn't know how many men were inside the house, so they split up to surround them as two went out the back and two went through the front. Detective Carl opened the front door sneaking his right arm on the handle whilst he was hiding behind the wall. He leaned around the corner and aimed his gun but could see nothing in the house. Carl entered the house into the living room and seconds later Nike fired his gun at Carl from behind the sofa and caught him on the arm. Carl took cover quickly and waited until Nike's gun ran out, and when it did, Carl arrested Nike and put on the hand cuffs.

Luke was in the kitchen with Wayne and they both were surrounded as all the four officers had them caught. Luke started to shake because he knew he was done for. He dropped his gun and put his hands up to give himself in to the police. But Wayne wasn't having that, he saw that as a coward's way out so then he shot Luke from behind. Now there was only Wayne left but by him holding Michelle hostage with a gun at her head, he was not making it easy for the police.

He warned them that if they came anywhere closer, he would pull the trigger and they would watch an innocent woman die. So for that reason, the police agreed to stay where they were. Wayne then told them to drop their weapons as well. However, PC Griffin aimed his gun at the side of Wayne's head and just waited for Wayne to turn his head for him to get a clear shot.

When PC Griffin got a clear shot on Wayne, he pulled the trigger and shot him on the head to save Michelle.

"Are you OK?" Carl asked Michelle. But she was in so much shock she couldn't even speak. When Michelle took a d e e p breath and managed to calm herself down, she told the police that she was fine and she thanked them for saving her life.

With no further enquiries, the police left Michelle's house and headed back to the station. Barry drove Pavilo to his house and headed to Michelle's with Lucas. When Barry got to the house Michelle heard their car approach so she looked out the window and could see Barry's car. She opened the door and let them both inside the house, and as Lucas got inside the house, he felt so bad as he couldn't believe what those men had done. They had smashed up everything in the house and left a mess on the floor.

Michelle saw Barry looking down at the man who attacked her in the kitchen and she asked him what was going on.

"They came into my house, I don't know who they were or what they wanted, but they ruined everything. When the police came, this man thought that I called them and he held his gun at me, I thought he was going to kill me. Who are these men?" Michelle asked.

Barry told Michelle, "They were Loki's men. I think it's time me and Lucas had some explaining to do."

Barry told Lucas and Michelle to sit at the table together; he made a cup for Michelle and himself and then started explaining to Michelle what really was going on.

Barry – "Lucas has got himself involved in a drug gang. But it's much worse than I hoped, it's Loki. The same guy I got involved with. They're trying to get Lucas to sell drugs but Lucas is refusing to do so and because of that, they're forcing him to buy the drugs and charging him more than the amount he'd get by selling. Loki will hurt anyone who fails to pay up. And because Lucas was never going to give him the money, he sent his men to kill you. I was the one that called the police, and he is not going to stop until he gets his money."

After Michelle heard everything, she really started to stress out, she couldn't believe everything that she heard.

"This is a dream; this can't be real? Drugs! Have you lost your mind? How much are they asking for?" Michelle asked. Lucas quietly told his mum that these smugglers wanted thirty grand off of him, and Michelle was stressing out. She got herself a glass of water to calm her nerves and asked how Lucas got into this mess.

Lucas explained everything to his mum how this all happened' it started when Lucas met these four men on bikes walking home from school. He walked down the high street and walked through the alley way which was where he met them.

The men acted as though they were friendly and Lucas thought he had met himself a group of friends until one day they showed him what they really drew him in for. They held out bags full of drugs and kept persuading Lucas to take some. Lucas then realised who these men really were and what a bad situation he had drawn himself into. Barry left the table and left Lucas and Michelle in peace as he went to get his jacket.

"Wait! Where're you going?" Lucas asked.

"You know where. I have to go and make sure these guys never bother us or anyone again. You stay here; you've got a lot to discuss with her. I'll be back," Barry said.

He went to his car and headed back to his apartment, he thought that it was time to set things straight.

He got his computer and started doing some detective work. He searched through every drug-dealing criminal that he had faced, even some of the ones that he had killed. Barry stayed up all night searching for info, he had typed up almost every criminal that he had met but couldn't find anything, even with Loki's name. On the next morning, someone knocked at the door, Barry went to answer and as he opened, he straightaway noticed that it was Lucas.

Barry – "What're you doing here? I thought I told you to stay at home with your mum?"

Lucas – "Oh, mum can look after herself. She needs a bit of time alone to think things through. Besides you need my help!"

Barry – "Do I now, what makes you say that?"

Lucas – "I know where Loki's main building is. All these nightclubs that they all kept saying, they were never

72

their main areas. They were just used as a place to do dealings. With so many people in a night getting drunk off their heads, they found clubs such handy places to draw more people in to the gang or to sell the drugs."

Barry told Lucas to guide him the way to the building as they zoomed into the car and went off. Lucas showed Barry the way to Loki's hide out, leading him into Paddington. The building itself was called The Recommendation and when the boys pulled over, they could see that there were men on guard outside. Barry picked up the mobile and texted Loki to let him know that he was outside the building. Loki responded to the text and told Barry to make his way up; he told him that he was on the sixtieth floor which was the top. Loki had men all around the building and he told them to bring Barry up to the office.

Barry got out of his car and approached the building with Lucas. As they entered their way in, Loki's guards just stood at the door and allowed them to enter. They went inside the building and straightaway three men approached them. Nylon was one of the dealers, he told Barry that Loki was expecting him and they took him and Lucas to Loki's office in the elevator.

Nylon knocked on Loki's door and showed Barry in. But as the door opened, they could see that Loki was having a big meeting with people. Loki finished the meeting and let all the people out so that he could have a nice discussion with Barry. When all the people were gone, Loki let Barry in his office but told Nylon to keep Lucas company as he wanted to have a chat with Barry alone.

"Nylon, keep our friend Lucas company, me and Barry need to have a private chat in my office," he said as he shut the door behind him.

Loki – "So you to still think you can stop this, hey?"

Barry – "You think I'm just going to stay at home and let you carry on. Taking lives from innocent people, smuggling harmful substances around the country."

Loki –. "You know, sometimes I wonder if this is just a game to you Barry. I've offered you my life a couple of times and you wouldn't take it because you know you won't, and as for this business, it's time you finally realised the truth."

Loki turned on the projector screen in the room and showed Barry all the people that he had been video chatting from other countries. Loki had turned the screen off so he wasn't online and in the conversation, but the rest of them had carried on discussing business. When Loki turned on the screen, he was back online and in the conversation with all the other countries, he showed Barry all the other countries that were in the drug trade dealing together. All these people from the countries were people that hated the government and were earning fortunes by dealing drugs around the world. Loki introduced Barry to all the men online and when Barry saw all the eight other countries that were involved he was stunned. Russia, China, South Korea, Germany, France, USA, Japan and Canada were all involved in the trade deal with Loki, but Loki didn't have much of a conversation, he just introduced Barry and told them all before he switched off the screen.

Loki – "Do you see now, Barry? No matter how much you try, you cannot stop the drug trade, it's a business. Not even the police can stop it, It's all over the world, Barry. They could go out for days arresting dealers that have been involved in this but that wouldn't stop anything. All that would happen is more would come to replace them. You won't believe me when I say this, but it is just the same as the government. Because if someone just goes out there and assassinates the Prime Minister right now, what good would that do? Nothing! All that would happen is that person would be locked up and they'd just find a replacement.

The only difference is we are loyal; we are normal people. As for them, they're mentally ill, they have problems. They think they're the gods of this planet, standing there on stage, having their voices heard every day whilst we're all working our butts off to earn a living. Its slavery, Barry, that's what it is. They get their tax collectors to make us pay half of our earnings back to them and what for? People say it's to help the government improve our country and develop a better world for our nation, but everything they say is nothing but lies for money. They don't care about us; they leave people to rot on the streets, they increase the bills when they want, so people stress out until it becomes too much and leads to suicide. They're nothing but pig-headed crooks. It's them who are the real criminals. not us. It's them who make people like me who we are now, but the public just doesn't see it that way. They see their own people as the main villains. That's why all these people you see have gone to drug-dealing. Like I said to you, Barry, they rob us then we rob them, fair is fair, equal rights."

Barry wasn't convinced by Loki's words. He still deeply felt that Loki had to pay for what he did to him and all the guys he had met.

"You ruined my life, Loki. I can't let you get away with that. You set me up and now you must pay!" Barry said. But Loki corrected him and told him that it wasn't actually him who set him up on getting caught by the police. He had someone who wanted to see Barry, and that person was someone he knew well. Loki called the man on the phone to come in the office and a soon as he entered Barry was gob smacked as he couldn't believe what was happening. The man who came in was one of Barry's close Police colleagues PC Derek Stan. He came into the room with a big smile on his face and said, "Hello, Barry, how wonderful it is to see you again." Barry just looked at Derek in shame as he asked him why he would do this, but Barry didn't even know half of what was going on.

Barry – "Why, Derek? Why mess things up for yourself by joining the drug trade? You saw what it did to me, and the same will happen to you."

Derek – "No, Barry, you think you know what's going on here, but the truth is you know nothing. Let me tell you the real truth about what happened shall I? Loki wasn't the one who set you up the day you got caught, it was me!"

Derek – "I was never really a real copper; I only took the role as a police officer just to spy on them, and also keep my eyes on you. I was like you Barry, just instead of an undercover police officer, I was what we'd call an undercover smuggler listening to every last word the police had to say and getting rid of the main man. I knew that you were a threat to us, you might act like a tough guy Barry but the truth is you're just like a soft sponge inside. You feel for all these people that you see having their lives ruined by drug gangs, and violence and you blame Loki for it all."

Derek – "You think I'd really work for the police? You've seen what they're like; I saw your reaction with Glen. They're greedy; they think they're on top of everyone just because they can get away with murder. Do you know why they don't bother solving things out for the public when they're asked? It's not just because of paperwork, it's because they get paid huge amounts from the government and for that reason they can't be bothered. They just make stories up like politics as they go along."

Derek – "All you kept going on about was Loki. Let's get Loki, I need to catch Loki! I could tell you meant every word of that, so you needed to be stopped. Because I knew if I didn't stop you, you'd be here ruining our business, destroying our buildings, and killing off our men, like you've already started doing now. So when I heard from Loki that you made a deal with him, I knew that was a bad idea so I set you up. I delivered a whole load of drugs to your door and spoke to Glen on the next day before I arrived with the police at your house and got you caught. When I heard you had been sentenced for seventeen years, don't get me wrong I felt sorry for you, but I also felt pleased as I thought you would no longer be in the way of our business."

Derek told Barry that was all in the past and that now he should start over. But Barry was fuming as Derek had ruined his life as soon as he set him in prison. Barry asked the guys where Lucas was and so Derek straightaway called the guys on the radio to bring the boy to the office. They brought the boy into the office and Derek told Barry that it was time to move on from the past and start fresh. He had second thoughts that maybe he could get Barry involved in the drug gang as he now had got his mind off of Loki.

While Loki stayed behind in The Recommendation, Derek had something to show him and Lucas. He led them down stairs out of the building and into his vehicle. Derek got them in his car and drove them all the way from London to Felixstowe where all the drugs were delivered. As they headed on their way, Barry got his phone out quietly and sent a message to Zacos saying "now." Zacos and his men were outside The Recommendation building waiting for the signal from Barry, as they were about to give these low life smugglers a taste of their own medicine. There were four cars waiting outside as Zacos had twelve armed men with him, including Pavilo. When Zacos received the text from Lucas they drove straight through the gates and started shooting thugs. The guys took cover as close as they could to the building, hiding behind vehicles and behind walls. When they shot the two guards it wasn't long before more dealers came out and the gun fight began.

After 30 minutes of shooting, Zacos and his men were in trouble, they were outnumbered and low on ammo. They ran back to the car quickly for their lives although some of them got shot on the way. All the guys went back in the car and asked Zacos what to do as they were now surrounded. Zacos then briefed on his oxygen machine and thought of an idea. He called Pavilo over and told him straight what he needed him to do, but he knew Pavilo wasn't going to like it.

Zacos – "Listen, we have only one option now before we all die. As soon I drive into that building, you must shoot my tank straightaway and blow them all up. You're the only one who can do this Pavi, you're the one with long range, you must!"

Pavilo – 'Are you crazy! I won't do that. Do you realise how much pain and suffering I've had since I took that girls life? I'm not a killer Zacos, I will not do it."

Zacos – "I know you're not a killer, Pavilo, but do you think I really enjoy spending the rest of my life breathing through a tube every day? You and all these guys, you got the time in your life to make things right. Me, I'm just an old man now Pavilo my time has come. Now do this and save yourself and these guys before we all die. Remember, you're not being a killer here, Pavilo, you do this and you'll be a hero, because you're going to stop these low lives from ruining anyone else's life. Ready?"

Pavilo nodded his headed and waited for Zacos to go. Zacos drove the car into the wall of the building and closed his eyes as he knew this was the end for him at any moment. Pavilo aimed the gun at the oxygen tank in the boot of the car and when he got a clear shot, he quickly pulled the trigger causing the car to blow up in flames. When the car went off, it destroyed the entrance to the building and all the dealers that came out shooting were killed. The entire ground floor was destroyed as there was nothing but flames and the fire was spreading fast all the way to the third floor.

Loki heard the blast and wondered what was going on so he contacted his pal Shane Reccenchie on the radio to ask what was going on and he told him that the building had been blown up and was now on fire from the 4th floor. But Pavilo and the guys couldn't care less about what'd happen to them as they watched the building burn they looked at Zacos's car and bowed as this was more a sad moment because they had just lost a good friend.

After a few minutes of paying their respects to Zacos, the guys went in their cars and headed back home, but some of them had to make their own way back as they had now lost a vehicle and there were too many of them. Meanwhile, in

Felixstowe, Derek reached his destination and took Barry to the Felixstowe port where all the freights were delivered from abroad by the cargo ships and loaded onto the trains. Barry could see that there was a whole load of men unloading freights from the cargo onto the train, and Derek had a surprise to show him. He showed Barry up onto the ship and opened one of the freights to show him what it actually was that was being loaded. Inside the freight were loads of cardboard boxes, Derek opened one of the boxes and grabbed out a wrapped-up bag that was filled with cocaine. There were six bags full of cocaine in the box and each weighed a pound.

When Derek had finally shown Barry what was being delivered around the country, he put the drug back into the box and said to Barry, "In case you think of stopping us, I should warn you that literally half of this entire train is filled with drugs with all these personal belongings to the public. If you stop us, you'll stop the public from receiving their gifts."

They got off the cargo ship and then Derek introduced Barry and Lucas to Fellini Miller. Mr Miller was also a member of the drug gang and was in charge of the gang loading the drugs from the cargo onto the train. Derek asked Miller if the train was ready to go and Miller told him that they had only one freight left to load before the train leaves.

But just then, Barry received a text from the guys telling him that The Recommendation was destroyed, and so then as Barry thought to himself that because Derek had no more reinforces to call from, it was now the chance for him to defeat Derek and stop that train from leaving before any more lives were harmed. Barry and Lucas hid from Derek behind one of the freights and Barry told Lucas to stay out of sight while he went after Derek. If anyone spotted Lucas, Barry told him to run or call him for help.

Barry went to stop Derek as he started taking down his men one by one. He picked up one of the guns and carried on searching round the whole port. Derek noticed that Barry had run off with Lucas and when he spotted some of his men lying on the floor unconscious he just said to himself, "My, my, my. Barry, you just don't know when to quit do you?" The last freight was loaded onto the train and so Miller pulled the switch to let the train go.

"What do you think you're going to do now, Barry? The train has already left there's no way of stopping it now!" Derek shouted, and straightaway gunshots were fired. Derek rushed into cover and then leaned around the corner as he thought that was Barry shooting at him, but as he looked he couldn't see anything. He walked further on and called Miller but got no response and when he went towards the office, he noticed that Miller had been shot.

Derek went in the CLS truck and drove after Barry. But when Barry noticed that the train was already leaving, he ran the fastest he ever could to catch it and he jumped onto the last car before it left the terminal. Derek couldn't find Barry anywhere at the port and started to get really annoyed. But then he looked at the train and as he watched it go by he could see Barry leaning on board the last car of the train.

Derek was furious; he hurried down the railway in the CLS truck and went straight after the train shooting his gun straight at Barry. As the gun went off and Derek got closer Barry started climbing on the freight. He jumped up and grabbed the top and quickly started to climb before Derek arrived, but he found it a real struggle as the train was starting to go at a pace. Barry jumped from one freight to another making his way over to the locomotive.

As he made his way over, gun shots were still firing, and when he turned around, he could see that Derek was now on the train and just on his tail. Barry made his way to the locomotive and just stood there waiting for Derek, struggling to hold his balance as the train was now going at full speed. When Derek got on the locomotive, he threw his gun off the train and held his fists up at Barry as he said, "This is it, Barry, I gave you a choice and you denied it. Now here's where we draw a line. Let's see who's a real man, shall we? And can stay on a train at 120 mph, the first one who falls will die."

Barry dropped his gun and just said to Derek, "With pleasure!" holding his fists towards Derek with a displeased look. These two men fought for ages on the train, they were so equal they just kept punching one after another. Derek pinned Barry down on the edge of the train, holding his hands as tight as possible to his neck trying to strangle him to death. Barry kept hitting Derek on the face to get loose; he gave it more force going harder and harder until Derek would let go. Barry quickly got up and because he hit him so hard, Derek was still down. He just looked at Barry and said, "What're you going to do, Barry? Finish me?" he asked but Barry said nothing.

Barry just held out his hand at Derek making him think he was offering him a hand up, but a soon as Derek took his hand Barry kneeled towards him and whispered in his ear "See you in hell!" before he kicked him off board in front of the train to get crushed.

As soon as Derek was gone, Barry climbed down inside the locomotive, and quickly pulled the brakes to stop the train. He put the train into reverse so that he could get it all the way back to the port. When Barry got to the port, he called Lucas over and told all the workers to stop loading the freights. The workers thought that Barry was crazy as they didn't know that they had illegal substances inside so when Barry told them they stopped. Barry drove Lucas home in Derek's car and whilst they were on their long journey back to Sidcup Lucas dialled the emergency contact number and got in touch with the Felixstowe Police Station and told them about all the illegal substances that were getting delivered in freights with people's belongings.

So then, an hour later, the Police got to the Felixstowe port and closed it all off. All the workers were sent home and no ships or trains were allowed to approach the premises until the port had reopened. The police had to open every single port, including the ones on the train and the ship. This was going to take them weeks to search every container and a long while for the port to reopen.

One week later, the Metropolitan Police received all the info on what happened in Felixstowe from the Felixstowe Police and when they found out what had happened to Derek and the other dealers, they went over to Barry's apartment and arrested him. He was kept at the station for a month until he was back in court at the Old Bailey. Judge J Baldwin was surprised to see Barry back in his court room and with all the metropolitan police watching Barry felt that maybe now is his last chance to apologise and wish forgiveness from all his friends. When Barry stood there next to the judge in front of everyone, he swore that everything he said would be the truth and the truth only. The prosecutor asked him if he killed Derek and all those that were in his name and Barry, without any hesitation, just said yes. After admitting to all the men that he had killed, Barry spoke to the whole crowd in court saying.

Barry – "All the things I have done, I am not proud of. Tell you the truth, I hate myself for it, I really do. Derek was right on one thing, I may act hard, brutal and nasty, but deep inside I am just a week, pathetic old man. I was a man, who thought that he could do everything by himself, a man who would take advice from no one, and now I have shown my sins. And from this I have learnt that listening to your own advice is the wrong move but getting help from other people will lead you to the goal. People say life is a mystery, like a pathway, but I'd say it's more like a maze, a jungle, or a cave. You're standing there waiting to find out what you're headed to next. If you've chosen the wrong path then you head to danger. But when you get help from other people, it's much easier to get yourself on the right track and that's what I didn't do; listen! That's what got me into this mess, so it was my own fault, I couldn't allow a young boy to end up in the same position as me so that's why I did what I did and saved him!"

When Barry had finished, he looked up at his old friend Carl. He knew he must be feeling low as when Barry went to prison Derek was his next closest mate. Never did he know until now that Derek was a spy member of the drug gang. He looked at Carl and said to him, "Carl! Words probably don't describe what you're going through. But all I can say is I'm truly deeply sorry. Even if you may or may not forgive me, I just want you to know that it's been an honour having you as my best friend and it always will be."

Lucas took the stage and gave his announcements to the court on what Barry had done. He told the court everything that Barry had done and what a hero he was to him as without Barry, Lucas wouldn't be around.

"Barry has saved my life on numerous occasions; he is a hero to me and a well-known true friend. When I first started meeting these guys, I didn't know anything about this drug dealership, I thought they were just a group on guys. Barry must've known what these guys were like from his previous encounter, I was so scared that I didn't know what to do. I was worried that if I told mum she'd call the police and probably never want to speak to me again, if I called the police I'd be arrested. And they were forcing me to sell drugs to people for money which I refused to do but when they didn't get their money, they came after me and tried to kill me. That's when Barry came along and saved my life."

When Lucas finished his speech, it was time for the jury to make a decision on what they were going to do to Barry. But as the judge started to speak, a loud noise came from out of the door. The doors pushed open and Pavilo entered the room, he said to the judge, "Your honour, I'd like to make an announcement about the witness if you wouldn't mind?" The judge nodded his head and pointed him to the stage, he told Pavilo to make it a quick one as it was getting close to time. "You don't know me, but I'm an old friend of Barry's. Barry had another old friend as well, who's sadly not here now, but he also had his life ruined by these low life criminals. They shot him cold, and he survived but because his lung was damaged, he had to spend the rest of his life on a machine. As for me, they knew I was too kind-hearted and they couldn't allow for me to be in their filthy crew. So they took an innocent young girl and forced me to shoot her giving me a gun in my hand.

Having a gun pointed at my head, if I refused, I was so scared for my life, I just aimed it, closed my eyes and there it happened. I killed an innocent young woman because I was too scared to let my own life go and ever since then I just started drinking myself to death because I was full of shame and guilt and I just couldn't take it. No one has ever been able to stop me from drinking but Barry there's something about him, it's like he knows what's wrong with you and with one small word he can get you inside. Barry knows what these animals are doing to people and he knows how to give people hope and a new way of life before it's too late."

Pavilo went out the door and headed up the stairs into the audience. Now was the time for the judge and jury to make a decision. When the judge asked the jury, every one claimed Barry guilty for the murders that he had committed. However, after hearing the reactions from Pavilo and Lucas, the judge had to have a big think on what to do as he could tell that this was a crime on saving innocents from killing baddies.

Judge J Baldwin – "Well then, Barry, you've heard from the jury. However, after hearing all that from your friends, it sounds like you were being a hero. You saved the boy's life and Pavilo's too. Also, if I'm not mistaken, if it weren't for you the Metropolitan Police would never have known about Derek's secret undercover scheme so you've also saved them as well.

So for that reason, I am not sending you in prison for this time being. You will be going on community service for three years where you'll be doing volunteer working and helping the public. A world of warning Barry, a lot of people might dislike my decision so consider yourself lucky. This means that you're not allowed to work anywhere else whilst on the community. If you fail to attempt this, or let me down at all, you will be sent straight back in the cage!" So then the court ended and some people were left pleased, others were left annoyed.

"So was that a good decision from the judge, can Barry really put a mend to his life or should he have gone back in prison. Find out what happens next as the story follows on in EX COP 2!"